THE DEATH DEALERS
Fantastic Sleuths
Battling
Diabolical Villains

Pulp Classics # 21

R. Reginald

the Borgo Press

San Bernardino, California
MCMLXXX

Library of Congress Cataloging in Publication Data
Main entry under title:

The Death dealers.

  (Pulp classics ; no. 21)
  CONTENTS: Chadwick, P. Doctor Zero.--Kelley, B. J.
The Death Dealer.--Cooley, D. G. Merchants of panic.--
[etc.]
  1. Horror tales, American. 2. Detective and
mystery stories, American.
PS648.H6D4   813'.0872'08   80-8667
ISBN 0-89370-099-1
ISBN 0-89370-097-5 (pbk.)

CONTENTS

Doctor Zero

Whose Scientific Cunning Created a New Kind of Death

The night glowed purple!

A "Wade Hammond" Novelet

By PAUL CHADWICK

Author of "Skyscraper Horror,"
"The Corpses' Carnival," etc.

*From the black vault of the heavens came a hissing ball of purple light. As if
possessing uncanny human intelligence, it rocketed straight for the victim
it had marked. The police were helpless before that sinister sphere of
Doctor Zero's. And now, Wade Hammond, explorer and criminal
investigator, had stepped into the eerie glow of the
Purple Peril.*

CHAPTER I

DEATH'S MESSENGER

"WHAT'S that?" Detective O'Conner's voice was a nasal bleat. His eyes bulged under the brim of his soft felt hat. His dank cigarette slipped from trembling fingers. He stared off into the darkness across the wide lawn of Gordon Munn's suburban house.

A fellow dick, one of a cordon thrown around the place to protect its owner from the mysterious menace of "Doctor Zero," shook his head. He also was staring in amazement.

"It looks like a rocket," O'Conner went on. "No—it's coming nearer. Hell, we ought to warn Munn."

He started off across the lawn at a lumbering gallop. The sky behind him had turned into a vivid violet. There was a strange, hissing sound in the air. A fantastic ball of eerie purple light was descending toward the house. It moved as though some unseen power were directing it—moved with horrible certainty toward the window of Munn's study.

O'Conner waved his arms and shouted. At that instant the ball of purple fire touched the window panes. There came a noise like the crack of a giant whip, then a deafening concussion that shattered every piece of glass in the sash, sending gleaming slivers inward and outward and searing the boards along the side of the house.

A stinging needle of glass struck the detective. He bawled loudly and clutched at his face. Men were shouting to each other out on the lawn now. A half score of plainclothes men came running up, converging on the house from three sides. A babble of voices sounded.

"It's a bomb—who threw it?"

"See if Munn's hurt!"

"Turn in an alarm!"

Questions, orders and explanations tumbled over each other. Then O'Conner spoke again. "There's another one coming—look out!"

The ball this time seemed to swoop out of the black night sky like a sinister will-o'-the-wisp. It appeared first as a pinpoint of light, hardly distinguishable from the stars. It might have been a shooting star as it flashed across the sky.

But as it came nearer its speed diminished. Again there was that uncanny effect of diabolical intelligence. The hissing, whirling ball of purple fire followed its predecessor. The first one had cleared the way. The second plunged through the gaping hole of the shattered window while detectives screamed a warning.

They heard a muffled explosion this time. Lurid tongues of light speared from the window, dancing like an aurora borealis. The room inside looked for a moment to those staring from the darkness like the mouth of some fantastic inferno such as the hand of a Doré might have depicted.

Above the noise of the concussion they heard a single, horrible cry. Then blackness descended and the night seemed to close in, bringing silence with it. The voices of the detectives grew hushed with amazement and the awe of the unknown.

O'Conner entered the house with his men behind him. They found the servants huddled into a frightened, whispering group near the hall stairway. Then they climbed to the floor above, entered Munn's study and swore harshly at the thing they saw.

Gordon Munn, director in a great and powerful bank, and shareholder in a dozen corporations, was lying face downward on the rug, his clothing in singed tatters, his body twisted and blackened into an unsightly caricature of a man.

THREE miles away in Wade Hammond's apartment the French-type telephone jangled into life. The curio-lined walls of the living room threw the sound back harshly. The stuffed heads of big game, collected in a dozen far corners of the world, stared down with unblinking eyes as though listening.

Hammond, sprawled in a big armchair, dropped his cigarette into an ash tray, untangled his legs and got up. He crossed the room in four quick strides. Ten years of newspaper and police work had taught him to answer phone calls promptly. But his deeply tanned face was impassive as he picked the instrument up. People were always giving him a buzz for one thing or another. His lips below their thin mustache line barely moved in the mouthpiece.

"Hello! Hammond speaking."

Words came from the other end of the wire in an excited quaver.

"Listen, Hammond—this is Sergeant O'Conner. All hell's popping. Gordon Munn's been knocked off in spite of us."

"Gordon Munn?"

"Yeah—the bank man. You know who he is. Can you come out? The chief wants you. Follow Parkway Boulevard and make the first turn to your right. It's the big yellow house with the iron fence in front of it. Step on it!"

"O. K." Again Wade's lips moved. No use asking questions now. The dope would come later after he got to the scene of the killing. When Inspector Thompson called, it meant there was a tough nut to be cracked.

Wade's movements in the next few seconds were like those of a well-oiled machine—a machine taut with blued steel springs and rapid-action mechanism. But the springs were his muscles and the motivating mechanism was the flashing power of his quick-fire brain.

He threw off his dressing gown, pulled on a coat, stuck his feet into shoes, shoved a flat, wicked-looking automatic into his pocket and grabbed a hat. Three minutes later wind was whistling past the radiator cap on the battleship nose of his sport roadster.

He held the button on the steering column down at every intersection, defying traffic lights and making the night raucous. Twice he lifted a gloved hand at red-faced cops who stared belligerently. The fighting expressions left their faces when they saw who it was.

It was known that Wade Hammond carried a special investigator's card bearing the signature of the commissioner himself. It was also known that it didn't pay to interfere with him.

He swung into the driveway of the Munn estate. Gravel snapped under fat balloon tires as he roared up to the front steps. The headlights of his car goggled into the shrubbery. Almost before the motor stopped ticking over he was up the steps and inside the house.

Inspector Thompson, the grizzled chief of the City Homicide Bureau, was coming forward through the hallway to meet him, his expression owlish as always.

"Sorry to dig you out of bed, Hammond. They caught me at a banquet—right in the middle of a steak, smothered with onions. It's tough when a fellah can't enjoy his grub."

"Tough is right. What's going on here, chief? O'Conner sounded fussed when he called."

"Why wouldn't he? Didn't he tell you Munn had got his?"

Wade nodded grimly. Thompson's features suddenly reddened. His voice was thick with anger.

"I'm going to burn up somebody for this. Munn asked for protection. I sent enough men out here to guard the sub-treasury—and they let that devil rub him out anyway."

"Who?"

"Doctor Zero."

Wade shook his head.

"You'll have to start **from**

scratch, chief. You've been holding out on me. Who's Doctor Zero?"

"I wish I knew. That's what he calls himself. He tried to get cash out of Munn—sent him a scare letter—and a bundle."

"A bundle? What was in it?"

"Come here, I'll show you."

THOMPSON turned and Wade followed him. They climbed to the second floor, to the room where Munn had been killed. The place was filled with headquarters' men; detectives, the medical examiner and his assistant, and experts from the bomb squad. Munn was still sprawled on the rug near a table, pieces of glass all around him from the shattered window. Thompson spoke in Wade's ear.

"Look here."

The inspector was lifting an odd-looking contraption from a pasteboard box. There was a handful of thin, collapsed rubber; a small metal ball attached to it, and a long brass cylinder with a tube at its end stoppered by a brass valve.

"What is it—a bomb?" Wade spoke grimly.

"No, a balloon, Hammond—with a tank of compressed gas to fill it, and a place to put the cash."

"A present from Doctor Zero, eh?"

"Yeah. Munn was supposed to put fifty thousand dollars into that tea-ball gadget and send the balloon up when it got dark. I don't know how the hell Zero expected to get it back. It might land any place within a thousand miles. He must be a nut."

Wade did not answer. He was looking interested, staring at the balloon keenly, and fingering the small round cash box. It was made of some light-weight metal. There was a coating on it. Some sort of waterproof paint apparently.

"Munn would have done better to have followed instructions," he said.

Thompson swore under his breath and nodded.

"He had plenty of dough, but he didn't want to send fifty thousand of it sky-hooting all over the landscape—you can't blame him. He sat tight and called on us. Now it'll get out that the department fell down on the job. It's going to raise a stink."

Wade fired a sudden question. "What sort of a bomb did Doctor Zero use and where did it come from?" Thompson shrugged. "Nobody knows yet. Carmichael and Parks are working on it now. The fellahs who saw it say it wasn't a bomb at all. It floated through the air, they say. It seemed to come from the sky—sort of purple fire."

Wade spoke quickly, his voice hard.

"This Doctor Zero is no nut, chief. You can bet on that. He must have known what he was doing when he sent that balloon. We've both heard of scientific criminals, and read yarns about them. Now we're up against one. It's the smartest extortion racket I've ever bumped into, with murder as a side line. Some guy who's half genius and half devil is behind this—and he must want the money bad."

Thompson grunted and Wade spoke again.

"We won't learn much here. That's a cinch. Mind if I go off with that balloon?"

"I can't let you, Hammond." Thompson spoke regretfully. "My men have got to have it to trace the material—see where it was bought."

Wade made an impatient gesture.

"They'll have a good time doing it. Let me have a few scrapings then. I think there's something queer here—and deep, too."

Inspector Thompson stared uncomprehendingly while Wade took a pen-knife from his pocket and scraped some of the paint and metal off the ball-like cash receptacle onto a paper. He stuffed this into his pocket and spoke slowly.

"That's the angle I'm going to work on first, chief. I got a hunch about something. I think—"

He stopped suddenly. A girl was standing in the door of the room; a girl with blonde hair, frightened eyes, and bloodless lips. She made a little whimpering sound in her throat, and moved forward; but a detective held her back.

"Better not look at him, miss. It won't do any good."

The girl burst into a spasm of crying, her slim shoulders shaking.

"That's Munn's daughter, Arlene," Thompson whispered. "She must have just come. We'll have to get her out."

Wade followed the inspector, and as they neared the doorway he saw a man standing behind the girl. Thompson was speaking in a kindly voice.

"We'd better go downstairs, Miss Munn. There was an explosion— you'd better remember your father the way he was."

HE led the girl gently out into the hall while Wade sized up her escort. The man was thin and aristocratic looking with features so clean-cut as to be almost harsh. He was dressed elegantly, and wore an aloof expression. Wade had seen the face somewhere before.

Arlene Munn recovered enough to introduce him when they got downstairs. The formalities had been bred into her.

"Professor Ornstein," she said. "We were dancing at the Belmont when they paged us—and told me about father." She choked again.

"I came here as fast as I could," Ornstein said. "It's a terrible thing. I'm awfully sorry." His words were sympathetic, but his tone sounded casual. Wade's thoughts were active, building up impressions, remembering scraps of information.

He had Professor Harold Ornstein checked now. The man was connected with the Technological Institute—a brilliant scientist specializing in physics; a dapper society light when he cared to be, and a person of independent means. It was an odd combination. Wade recalled Ornstein's name in connection with a recent breach-of-promise suit. The man, who was at least twenty years older than Arlene Munn, had a bad reputation with women. Science was his life work; philandering his recreation. He had won the Nobel Prize for his researches into the nature of matter, and the "ignoble" prize in his dealings with the ladies. Wade smiled grimly at the bad pun.

But he didn't like Ornstein, and sensed a certain hostility in the man. Still, the professor was a genius in his line. He might even be able to help in this strange case. Wade started to speak, but Arlene Munn interrupted, weeping again.

"I can't stand it!" she said. "I can't! Take me away from here, Harry."

"That's a good idea," said Inspector Thompson. "We can talk to you later, Miss Munn."

"I'll take her to her aunt's," said Ornstein smoothly. "She'll feel better when she's had a drink and quieted down a bit. If I can be of any service let me know."

The two of them moved toward the front door; Arlene slender and wilting, Ornstein tall and bland, looking somehow like a suave Satan.

"A pretty slick bird," said Thompson. "If there's science mixed up in this as you say, Hammond, we'd better check up on him. I wonder if he was at the Belmont with Miss Munn all evening?"

Thompson called one of his men and had a low-voiced conversation with him. Then he whirled, facing Wade and listening.

Shouts had suddenly come from outside, then the sound of two pistol shots in quick succession. Wade was already headed for the door.

"Come on, chief," he said. "This seems to be our busy night!"

CHAPTER II

A SPY IN THE DARK

WHEN Wade H a m m o n d reached the broad side veranda of Munn's house he saw three figures coming up the steps. Two of them were detectives. The man in the middle seemed to be their prisoner. They had him by the arms and were pushing him forcibly forward.

One of the detectives, a man with a red, perspiring face, turned to Inspector Thompson and spoke.

"We found this bird snooping around outside, chief. He started to run and Bill had to pull a gun on him. He's lucky he didn't get bumped off. He would have if I'd done the shooting."

"Bring him in the house," said Thompson. "Who is he?"

"You've got me, chief; but he looks like a bad actor."

The two plain-clothes m e n shoved their prisoner into the lighted hallway. Wade stared at the man sharply. He was young, somewhere in his early twenties apparently, and he had the gangling look of a student with bookish tendencies. This was accentuated by the heavy shell-rimmed spectacles he wore. His face had a sullen expression as he stood blinking his eyes in the light.

"What's your name?" asked Thompson harshly. "What were you doing out there on the lawn?"

The young man continued to blink. Then he spoke in a surly monotone.

"I was just looking around. I'm Zadok Smith."

"Looking around!" The inspector's voice was sarcastic. "What were you looking for—did you lose a nickel or something?"

Smith's face reddened. He pressed his lips together and shook his head. Thompson flared up.

"You won't talk, eh? You're one of those tight-lipped guys! Frisk him, Ed, and see if he's heeled."

The red-faced detective began going through Zadok Smith's pockets with professional thoroughness. He gave an excited exclamation as he drew something from the young man's coat where a conspicuous bulge had showed. It was an oblong leatherette case with two button fasteners. Thompson took it out of his hand and opened it while Wade stared over his shoulder.

Inside the case were two round glass dials with a knurled screw head in the center. Needle-shaped indicators behind the glass of the dials were quivering. Wade spoke tensely.

"That's a galvanometer, I think. The other's a compass. They seem to be hitched together. It's a funnylooking gadget."

"What's a galvanometer?" asked Thompson peevishly.

"It shows when there's an electric current," said Wade. "What were you doing with this thing, Smith?"

Smith stared at Wade as sullenly as he had at the inspector. "It's my business," he said. "I wasn't hurting anybody, was I?"

The cords in Inspector Thompson's neck swelled. "No?" he shouted. "Well—somebody hurt Gordon Munn here tonight—killed him! You've got a lot of explaining to do, Smith. You'd better answer our questions."

Wade nodded. "It'll save you trouble," he said. "Tell us what you know, Smith. You wouldn't be carrying that thing around if you weren't in on something. There's been a murder in this house—and murder can't be laughed off."

Smith's sullen face turned pale, but he maintained a stony silence. Wade shrugged. "Have it your own way. You'll talk later if you don't now."

"You bet he will," said Thompson angrily. "Take him down to headquarters, Ed. We can find a way to unbutton his lip down there."

Thompson, Wade saw, was still smarting under the knowledge that the police department had fallen down in its attempt to protect Munn. The inspector handed the leatherette case to one of the detectives.

"Give this to Carmichael and Parks. They're going down with that balloon contraption. They can take Smith along with them. Go out and see if anybody else is snooping around here."

The two detectives turned their prisoner over to Parks and Carmichael who were just coming down the stairs with the cardboard box containing the balloon. Wade spoke.

"I think I'll follow after them, chief. There's not much I can do here—and I'm curious about that gadget of Smith's. He wasn't carrying it just for fun."

Wade left the house with the two headquarters men and their prisoner. He had no clear picture of the crime in his mind as yet. He'd taken an active part in many other strange homicide cases; but this murder gave indications of being the most sinister and fantastic he'd ever bumped into. His mind reverted to the sprawled and blackened form of Gordon Munn and to the weeping figure of Arlene as he had first seen her in the doorway of the room where her father had met death. What human fiend was behind this? Who was Doctor Zero, and what did Zadok Smith know about the case that he was not willing to tell?

WADE was still asking himself these questions as the police car containing Parks, Carmichael and their prisoner turned out of the driveway. He followed it in his own

fast roadster. He wanted to be on hand when an expert in the criminal investigation bureau examined the instrument that Smith carried.

The tail-light of the police car stared unwinkingly out of the darkness ahead like the eye of some monster. They passed other rich men's estates; big houses set far back on well-kept lawns. An indefinable pall of horror seemed to blend with the shadows of the night.

The police car neared Parkway Boulevard with Wade's roadster a hundred feet behind. There were no other cars in sight. For a distance equaling two city blocks an embankment rose on either side of the road and the pole lights were spaced far apart.

Wade, occupied with his own thoughts, became aware suddenly of an unnatural glow on the distant horizon. Eerie reflections danced on the vibrating windshield of his roadster. His eyes, registering that glow and those faint reflections, telegraphed a warning to his subconscious mind. A sensation that was like the touch of chill fingers ran up his spine.

Then he cried out. The glow had deepened. It was concentrated in a pin-point of light like a shooting star —a star that was coming nearer and which shed a lurid, uncanny radiance.

Wade heard a sudden squeal of brakes ahead. Then a scream of human terror sounded followed by the noise of breaking glass. The police car swerved toward the side of the road, and, in the glare of his own car's headlights, Wade saw a gangling, bespectacled form jump from the auto in front of him.

He recognized it as Zadok Smith. He saw Smith stumble and drop to his knees. Pin-points of orange flame speared the darkness over his head as one of the detectives fired at the escaping prisoner. Then with an awkward leap Smith vanished into the shadows of the shrub-clothed embankment. Behind him the night was made ghastly by another unearthly scream.

The cause of Smith's terror was plain now. It wasn't his fear of the detectives' bullets. It was that dancing, fantastic pin-point of light which had now become a ball of purple fire headed straight toward the police car.

Wade heard one of the detectives shout a warning. They, too, had become aware of their peril. He saw the police car slew around and leap forward under the powerful thrust of a suddenly speeded motor.

Carmichael and Parks were trying to escape their doom.

Wade held his breath in horror. That lethal will-o'-the-wisp of light had changed its course now.

Some hidden intelligence acting through unknown physical forces was guilding it. It curved down in a hawklike swoop and followed the flying police car. For seconds that seemed to Wade like an eternity the terrible purple death pursued the speeding vehicle. It gained foot by foot, hovered over the car for an instant, then dropped like a falling meteor.

CHAPTER III

The Hand of Doctor Zero

WADE hadn't been on the scene when Munn was killed. But he heard a ripping, crackling burst of sound now. Then a terrible detonation blasted the air like an exploding bomb. He saw the top of the police car disintegrate in a pall of smoke and flame and zigzag streamers of light.

The swiftly moving car swerved from the road and headed up the embankment. He got a blurred glimpse of churning wheels, flying grass and thrashing bushes. Then the car swerved again in its erratic course. It turned turtle and came rolling back down the bank, where it lay, a smoking, twisted ruin beside the ditch.

The darkness of the night closed in, and Wade, feeling momentarily sick and weak for all the violent deaths he had seen in his life, brought his own roadster to a halt. He got out and walked forward unsteadily.

A man was lying dead in the roadway. It was one of the detectives, blown clear of the car when the fire ball had exploded, shattering the vehicle's top. Another man, whom Wade identified with a shudder, as Parks, was half pinned unde the battered wreckage. He, too, .ad been killed instantly.

Wade wiped beads of sweat from his forehead. The thing he had just seen was enough to shake any man's nerves. He remembered Zadok Smith then. Smith's frantic, terrified screams seemed still to ring in his ears. The young man had sensed his danger in time to jump from the car. His fear of the Purple Peril had driven him to risk the detectives' bullets.

Any evidence that the police car had contained had been destroyed.

Wade went back to his roadster and pulled a flashlight from under the front seat. He walked along the road to the spot where he'd seen Smith dive from the moving car. The dirt here was kicked up, showing the marks of Smith's knees. Up the embankment the branches of a number of bushes were broken, marking the trail of Smith's mad flight to escape death.

Then Wade caught his breath. His probing flashlight had revealed a gleam of metal in the shrubbery. He focused the beam and stooped down.

A small fraternity pin with some sort of cabalistic markings on it was lying at his feet. It had apparently been brushed from Zadok Smith's clothing. Wade picked it up and slipped it into his pocket.

There seemed to be little use in trying to follow Smith now. He should be a half mile away by this time. Terror had lent speed to his feet and the darkness would act as an all-concealing curtain.

Wade had been the sole witness of this grisly double murder. He lifted the body of the slain detective from the road and laid it beside the ruins of the police car.

Then he got into his roadster. He wanted to reach the nearest telephone quickly and let Inspector Thompson know that the sinister hand of Doctor Zero had brought death again.

He came to a filling station a mile down the road and stopped. There was a telephone in it. Wade's own voice was hoarse as he talked to the inspector over the wire.

Images of the killing he had witnessed and echoes of Zadok Smith's terrified screams still seemed to pulsate through his brain.

He felt as though the whole thing were a mad nightmare—but he knew it wasn't. In brief sentences he gave the details of the double murder to Thompson. He wound up with his own conclusions.

"We're dealing with a murderer who kills as unemotionally as a machine. He had nothing against Parks and Carmichael personally. He killed them because they carried evidence which might be dangerous."

Thompson's voice came back with a tremor in it.

"I can't have my men knocked off like this. We've got to find Doctor Zero."

WADE knew that the inspector wasn't taking the deaths of his two assistants lightly. The old crime-hunter concealed human emotion under a bluff, hard-boiled exterior. Parks and Carmichael had been with him for years.

"We'll find him," said Wade grimly. "There's a question mark after his name now—but it'll be a death s e n t e n c e before we're through."

"What'll you do next, Hammond —try to trace Smith?"

"Yès. Then I want to have a talk with Professor Ornstein. Have you any more dope on him, chief?"

"He stayed at the Belmont all evening with Miss Munn, as he told us. He left her only once to make a short telephone call. The house detective helped us check up on him. His alibi is water-tight."

"You and I've seen alibis break down before," Wade said. "Smith has an alibi, too, now. He was in the police car when the fire ball came. But he hasn't explained yet what he was doing prowling around Munn's house at the exact time of the murder."

"No—and here's another angle I've just thought of," said Thompson with a snap in his voice. "It didn't take more than three minutes for those balls that killed Munn to drop out of the air and explode. Ornstein's call was made somewhere around the same time. We don't know what sort of thing we're dealing with."

"Meaning?"

"Meaning that if there's science mixed up in this, as we think, we've got a tough job on our hands."

"Tough is right, chief." There was a humorless smile on Wade's face as he spoke.

It was after eleven when Wade drove to the campus of the Technological Institute and asked to be directed to Professor Ornstein's quarters. A night watchman stared at him, then pointed across the campus grounds to where lights were burning in the third story of a modernistic looking building.

"He's up there," the watchman said. "That's where he works. I saw his car go by ten minutes ago."

Wade examined the building that housed Ornstein's laboratory. It surprised him to find the man at work so late at night. Ornstein, he figured, must have left Arlene at her aunt's, then come back here.

And he must be a man with stout nerves to go calmly back to work after being at the scene of Munn's murder such a short time before.

A fire escape snaked down the side of the building, passing Professor Ornstein's windows. Wade noticed this and also saw the light in the front vestibule was burning. An automatic elevator connected with the various floors.

Wade took the elevator to Ornstein's floor and knocked. Ornstein himself came to the door. He had slipped a white coat over his evening clothes and looked trim and efficient. For a moment he stared at Wade blankly. Then he smiled in recognition.

"Hammond," he said. "I remember now. Come in."

"Sorry to interrupt your work, professor."

"Don't mind that. I'm always puttering around. I've got so I can't sleep if I don't amuse myself for a while before going to bed."

Wade studied the man for a second, then spoke.

"There was another murder after you left—a double one. Two detectives were killed. I want to ask you about a man named Zadok Smith. Ever hear of him?"

Ornstein whistled. Then an odd look came into his eyes. His sharp features had the satanic quality that Wade had noticed before.

"I know young Smith too well," Ornstein said. "He's a student here —one of Professor Hartz', specializing in mineralogy and analytical chemistry. Frankly I don't like him. He's an impertinent young devil. He has a habit of coming in here uninvited and making a nuisance of himself. I think he imagines he's spying on my work. He's annoyed Arlene, too."

"So Miss Munn knows him then?"

"Yes, slightly. She's good-hearted enough to tolerate his mooning around."

Wade nodded.

"Smith was found prowling outside the Munn house just after the murder. He had a queer instrument in his pocket—a compass and a galvanometer hitched together apparently. Two men started back to headquarters with him. Then another of those fire balls dropped out of the sky. Smith jumped and escaped and the two detectives were killed. Have you any theory, professor, as to what Smith might have been doing?"

A veil of suspicion seemed to drop over Ornstein's face for a moment. He laughed uneasily.

"You're connected with the police, Hammond," he said. "I wouldn't want to commit myself. I'd advise you, though, to find out all you can about Smith. Talk to Professor Hartz tomorrow. Smith's actions have certainly been queer."

"What about those fire balls?" said Wade. "I've got a theory that they may be electrical. You're a physicist. You ought to know."

"You mean you think they're controlled charges of static, like lightning?"

"Something of the sort."

"Look here!" Ornstein walked across the room quickly and opened a door. Through it Wade saw the complex paraphernalia of a modern scientific laboratory. There were shelves of chemicals, various electrical apparatus, including static machines of the Whymshurst type, Geissler tubes, and delicate instruments to demonstrate the composition of matter.

ORNSTEIN threw a small knife switch which sent current into the terminals of a ten-inch spark coil. The pungent, pleasant smell of ozone filled the air as miniature lightning flared between the gaps. A battery of foil-covered condensers were being charged. Close to them was an apparatus with adjustable electrodes. At the moment they were spaced four feet apart. The bottom one consisted of a copper plate two inches square.

"Watch," said Ornstein. "Here's lightning for you."

He reached into a box on a shelf and drew out a common walnut. He placed the nut on the copper electrode and stepped back.

"Call that nut a house," he said. "The electrode above is the sky. Now we have a thunderstorm. The electrode becomes a cloud."

He was speaking in his best classroom manner. Suddenly he turned off the overhead lights, then pressed another switch attached to a flexible cord.

There came a sharp, crackling report as a streak of violet light shot down from the top electrode. It struck the plate below in the millionth part of a second, passing through the walnut and sending shattered pieces of shell flying in all directions.

"In the General Electric Laboratories at Schenectady," said Ornstein, "they've made lightning that can shatter a block of hardwood. I use this little machine to give practical demonstrations to my students."

"There's more than one kind of lightning," said Wade. "This sort is known as chain, I believe. Could ball lightning be made in a laboratory, too, professor?"

Ornstein shot Wade a quick look, then smiled.

"Ball lightning is a rare phenomenon, Hammond. Its existence has been proven, but unusual atmospheric conditions cause it and it has never been reproduced artificially. Nothing is impossible, though, in the light of modern science. Lightning is the result of an electrical disturbance in the atoms of the air. The atoms in turn are made up of electrons. If a man found a way of controlling the electrons themselves he might do wonders. Professor Osterhout of Harvard estimates that there is enough potential elec-

tronic energy in a teaspoonful of water to drive a train across the continent."

Wade nodded, staring around him. There seemed to be other rooms connected with the main laboratory, but Ornstein didn't offer to show them. Wade sensed that the man was an adept at disguising his real thoughts. He was something of an enigma, always disarmingly pleasant.

Wade thanked the professor for his information and was preparing to go when the telephone in the outer room jangled. Ornstein picked the instrument up, then his face suddenly stiffened.

"My God—no!"

It was the first time Wade had seen any sign of emotion on Ornstein's part. The professor held the receiver to his ear for nearly a minute, then whirled around. He spoke tensely.

"Arlene—Miss Munn—has been kidnapped. I left her at her aunt's. She was going to spend the night there. A maid went to her room a few minutes ago and found her gone. The window was open and a ladder was leaning against it from the outside."

CHAPTER IV

The Sinister Visitor

ORNSTEIN began slipping out of his white jacket. He put on his overcoat, and in a moment he and Wade were descending in the elevator together. Two minutes later they turned out of the campus driveway in Wade's car and began speeding through the night toward the home of Arlene Munn's aunt.

When they reached it Wade saw more evidences of wealth, though the house wasn't quite as pretentious as Gordon Munn's. The dead man's sister, a large, florid woman of about forty, was in the drawing room with a bottle of smelling salts in her hand. She was close to hysteria, and the servants were running about panic stricken.

"Have you called the police?" asked Wade. The woman nodded. Her voice was a wail.

"This is terrible, terrible, terrible! Arlene came to me for protection—and now the poor girl is gone, and my poor dear brother, too!"

"She's not dead yet," said Wade. "We'll get her back."

With a flashlight in his hand he went outside. He saw that nothing had been touched. The window was still open in the room Arlene had been given for the night. The ladder still leaned against the house.

He walked carefully so as not to disturb any footprints before men from the bureau of identification came with their cameras and measuring instruments. He stooped over once, and a puzzled look flashed into his eyes. Two imprints of a girl's high-heeled slipper showed in a spot where the grass was thin. It looked to him as though Arlene Munn had walked calmly away from the house.

He waited till the police arrived, then left them to their methodical search for clews of the missing girl and drove Ornstein back to his quarters near the Technological Institute. Behind the professor's calm exterior Wade was aware of nervous tenseness. But Ornstein refused to admit that he was worried.

"Arlene has a lot of spirit," he said. "She can generally take care of herself."

THE next day Wade began systematically checking up on Zadok Smith. No trace of Smith had been found as yet. Arlene Munn hadn't been located, and the killing of Gordon Munn was still veiled in mystery.

The morning editions of the papers had run the stories of the Purple Peril and newsboys were still shouting in the streets. The whole city was agog with dread interest over the sinister series of murders which had taken place the previous night. The police department was coming in for a storm of criticism and Inspector Thompson was beside himself.

At a little after nine Wade Hammond drove into the campus grounds of the Technological Institute again. He went directly to the administration office and asked to see Professor Hartz.

"The police are anxious to check up on one of the students here named Zadok Smith," he told the girl at the desk. "Perhaps you've seen the morning papers. I believe Smith's name is mentioned."

The girl nodded. There was a scared look in her eyes.

"Professor Hartz has his laboratory in No. 14, Newton Hall," she said. "Follow the walk at the right as you go out."

Wade did as directed and found Hartz located in the top of one of the old brick buildings which had formed the nucleus of the institute before modern additions had been made. The Professor, with his woolly, white hair and his long, benign face, seemed as much a fixture as the building itself. He was dressed with comfortable simplicity in a baggy gray suit. The only touches of ornateness about him were the large diamond ring on his finger and the diamond scarf pin in his tie. These looked like heirlooms. A morning paper was carefully folded on the desk before him.

Wade introduced himself, displaying his special investigator's card.

"Sit down," said Hartz in a rumbling bass voice. "I suppose you've come about young Smith, one of my students. I see he's got his name in the papers." There was, thought Wade, a note of sadness in the professor's voice.

He nodded.

"Smith's wanted as a witness in connection with the murder of Gordon Munn and those two detectives. He's technically under arrest now. What's your opinion of his character?"

Hartz shook his white head slowly, and tapped the paper.

"They already have him branded as the murderer here," he said. "He was a brilliant student but an erratic one. I don't know what to say. It's hard to believe he'd do a thing like this."

"Where is he, then?" asked Wade. "What made him refuse to answer questions, and what was he doing on Munn's lawn?"

"I can't imagine where he is," said Hartz. "Curiosity might have led him to the scene of the murder; but none of it looks right."

"Professor Ornstein says that Smith is inclined to be impertinent," said Wade.

Hartz smiled and shrugged. His tone was slightly bitter.

"There's jealousy even in the halls of learning, Mr. Hammond. I sometimes think Professor Ornstein fears Smith as a future rival. Ornstein is a little erratic himself at times. He works too hard—often late at night. And he goes in for social life a great deal. We all wonder how he stands up under it."

After his interview with Professor Hartz, Wade got permission to search Zadok Smith's dormitory room. He hoped to find a diary, or papers that might throw more light on his character. But he found only an endless quantity of scientific notes written in Smith's painfully neat hand.

The room was neat, too, and Smith's few personal belongings had been chosen with care. He was evidently a serious-minded student who felt that he had a career before him.

Wade spent the rest of the day going over every detail of the case with Inspector Thompson.

A footprint had been found outside the window of Arlene Munn's room, just beside the ladder. It compared with another footprint discovered on the lawn of Munn's house. Both had been made by Zadok Smith apparently. This led to the belief that he had kidnapped her. A police dragnet was thrown out in an effort to trap the missing man.

Wade went back to his apartment late that evening and for a time paced the floor in deep thought.

He wondered grimly if the Purple Peril would strike again. Would the police find the man who hid behind the name of Doctor Zero before another victim had been claimed?

HE went to bed toward eleven that night and read a book for half an hour before dropping off to sleep. His brain was tired but restless from beating against the blank wall that had been reached in the Munn murder case.

Some time after midnight he woke up suddenly. His nerves were tingling oddly and he had a strange feeling—a sense that some one or something had been in the room with him while he slept.

Was it a dream brought on by the happenings of the past twenty-four hours? Or had some one really entered his apartment?

He got up, half ashamed of himself, and snapped on the lights. So far as he could see nothing had been disturbed. There was no one hiding in the place, and the doorway into the hall was locked. But he had used skeleton keys often enough himself to know that locks were not invulnerable. Some one *might* have entered.

He took the precaution now of snapping the special night latch on his door into place. Then he turned off the lights and went back to bed again.

But he couldn't sleep. Back in his mind was a feeling of uneasiness that refused to be shaken off. Something else was growing out of it—

an intangible sense of menace which deepened steadily like a thickening gray cloud.

He tried to ignore it, tried to tell himself that it was only his imagination playing tricks on him. But he kept on tossing restlessly.

He turned on his pillow for the tenth time and faced the window. Then suddenly his body tensed and his eyes grew wide with horror.

The oblong patch of sky that he could see was growing lighter, turning from the dark of night into a weird purple.

He leaped out of bed and reached the window with one bound. There, over the housetops, he could see it plainly now—a strange pin-point of light like a shooting star. As he watched, it gained in size, revolving itself into a whirling, eerie ball of fire.

The Purple Peril! The beacon of death itself!

With cold fingers clutching at his heart, Wade Hammond realized that the sinister ball of light was coming straight toward the window of his own apartment!

CHAPTER V

THE FIGURE IN BLACK

HE stared for seconds at the onrushing messenger of doom, unable to move. The ball came nearer, hovered overhead for an instant, then began a parabolic swoop toward earth. As it did so Wade's brain whipped the paralyzed muscles of his body into action.

He'd been a fighter all his life. Now he had a fight on his hands against the unknown forces of Doctor Zero.

He jumped to the window and slammed it shut, then turned and grabbed for his coat on the wall. He pulled it over his night clothes and reached the door in three strides. To stay in that room meant being blasted into eternity as Gordon Munn had been.

He snapped the lock open, stepped into the hallway and banged the door shut behind him. At the instant he did so the fire ball reached its mark.

There came again that sound like a giant whip being cracked, then a jarring concussion and the noise of shattering glass. The door strained on its hinges and slivers of glass tinkled against it.

Wade went down the apartment house stairs three at a time. He wanted to reach the street and see if another ball were coming. His brain was grappling with the mystery of the thing. It looked as though this visit had something to do with the deadly certainty of the fire ball's approach.

He ran across the dimly lighted foyer, stepped out into the street and looked up. A purple glow was visible again. Another of the lethal spheres was on its way. The street was deserted; but lights were beginning to show in nearby windows.

The glow deepened as Wade watched. Then the ball flashed into sight. It was coming across the housetops like a comet.

Wade stared, and his face whitened in horror. The ball hung overhead for an instant as the first one had done, then curved downward, a darting will-o'-the-wisp of destruction. But it wasn't headed for his window now. Its single glowing eye was moving straight toward him with terrible purpose, as though it possessed human intelligence.

Dampness broke out on Wade's forehead as he dashed headlong up the street. The ball dropped past his window and reached the spot where he had been a second before. It hung over the pavement, a glowing, incandescent globe of death. Then it floated after him in the same way that it had pursued the police car.

Screams came from those looking on overhead. Wade's breath whistled through his teeth in labored, horrified gasps. He zig-zagged, trying to escape the terror that followed him like Fate itself. He could feel the heat of it close behind him now. Any instant it might make contact with his body and accomplish its work of destruction. His feet seemed weighted with lead and his flapping overcoat hampered him.

Then he noticed something he hadn't been conscious of before. The left pocket of his coat seemed to sag. He thrust his hand in. His groping fingers closed over a piece of oblong metal, cold to the touch.

He hadn't put it there himself. What was it? Where had it come from? A strange look came into his eyes. He glanced over his shoulder and saw the purple ball of light close behind. He could hear the hissing, crackling noise it made as it swept through the air.

His hand came out of his pocket grasping the oblong piece of metal. With a fierce gesture he flung it away—and then a miracle seemed to happen.

The purple ball flashed off at a sudden tangent, hissing and whirling as it went, then dropped toward the spot where the strange metal had skidded to a stop.

Wade threw himself flat on the pavement as the air behind him seemed to explode with a roar. A wave of deafening sound came, followed by a battering current of wind. Stones and asphalt flew up in shattered pieces.

Where the metal had been all was darkness except for a few glowing sparks. These faded, and Wade, panting for breath, lifted himself to his feet.

He understood now. Some one *had* visited his room. Some one had dropped that piece of metal into his coat. Doctor Zero had visited him and marked him for death with this element that would attract the Purple Peril.

WADE went grimly back to his apartment with the ripping, crackling sound of the exploding fire ball still ringing in his ears. An alarm had been turned in by some one. He could hear a fire engine tearing up the street with its siren shrieking.

Bric-a-brac around the apartment had been broken by the explosion, and the telephone had been knocked off its table. Wade picked it up and called Inspector Thompson's number. Thompson would want to know that he was all right when reports of the attack came. The voice of the inspector reached him over the wire, sleepy and peevish.

"A hell of a time to get a man out of bed, Hammond."

"That's what I thought just now when Doctor Zero tried to bump me off," said Wade. "He pretty nearly succeeded, chief. My room here looks like a Texas cyclone had struck it."

He heard Thompson's gasp of surprise.

"He tried to get you, Hammond? Did you find out anything?"

"Yes, it's scientific stuff we're dealing with all right. I'm going to see some one about it."

"Who?"

"Professor Ornstein, chief. He can tell me a lot of things if he wants to, I'll bet."

Wade was dressed at the end of five minutes and on his way downstairs again. A huge crowd had collected in the street outside. People were staring up at his broken windows, at the shattered glass, and at the hole in the pavement.

He shouldered his way through them and got his roadster out of the garage. He shoved the accelerator down to the floor boards as he headed for the Technological Institute campus.

This time he parked his car outside the grounds and went toward Ornstein's laboratory without letting the night watchman see him. Lights were burning in Ornstein's place again. The professor was evidently hard at work.

Wade started to go in the front way; then hesitated and walked around to the fire escape. He wondered if he could jump up and reach the bottom ladder which was balanced and hung up from the ground by a weight. Then suddenly he shrank back into the shadows. He had heard the sound of footsteps on the iron rungs. Some one was coming down.

A moment more and Wade got a glimpse of a muffled black form descending the fire escape. As he watched, the man stepped on the ladder which automatically lowered itself as the weight went up. Rusty pivots squeaked in protest. The figure in black seemed hardly more than a sinister shadow. Who was he and what was he doing there?

Wade leaped forward. But a flower box close to the building and hidden by the darkness caught his foot. He half tripped over it, fell to his knees on the grass, and his shoe clattered on the box.

The man on the ladder gave a muttered curse. He leaped sidewise, landing on his feet on the grass below, then turned and darted away, blending with the night shadows before Wade could reach him.

Wade didn't try to give chase. There were a score of places on the campus where the black-robed stranger could hide. Wade ran into the building and pressed the button controlling the automatic elevator.

He waited impatiently while the car crawled up. Who was this stranger he had seen? Was it Ornstein himself?

He ran along the corridor and knocked loudly on Ornstein's door. He waited, knocked again, but there was no answer. Then he examined the door. He could see a thin glow of light coming from beneath it. Some one must be inside—

unless the man he had seen had been Ornstein—or unless—

Wade suddenly reached into his pocket and drew out a bunch of skeleton keys. They were marvelously delicate. One was more than a key. It was a complicated little tool with an adjusting screw at the end and teeth that could be set into any size lock. It was Wade's own invention.

He thrust it into the lock on Ornstein's door, turned the knurled screw head with sensitive fingers, and in a moment had the door open.

The lights in Ornstein's laboratory were still burning brightly. He stared around, then his eyes suddenly came to rest on the far end of the room. They widened in horror.

The huddled figure of Professor Ornstein was lying on the floor, his white coat thrown open. And at one side of the coat was a sinister circle of spreading crimson!

CHAPTER VI

A CRY FOR HELP

"MURDERED!" Wade's lips framed the words silently.

The man whom he had more than half suspected of being the killer was now lying dead at his feet! The handle of a small, sharp knife projected from Ornstein's side.

It was a knife that Wade remembered having seen on a shelf at the time of his former visit. Ornstein had used it as a paper cutter.

There were no signs of a struggle. The killer must have taken Ornstein by surprise.

Then Wade saw a half open door into the next room. He walked to it, opened it farther, and saw that it gave into a small laboratory with a window opening on a fire escape.

Something was lying in the center of the floor. It was a crumpled cambric handkerchief. He picked it up, then whistled. In one corner of the handkerchief were the initials "Z. S."

He went to the window and stared at it tensely. A square had been cut cleverly out of the pane and the glass pushed in so that some one could reach the lock. It had been done so neatly and quietly that Ornstein in the next room hadn't heard any one enter.

Wade examined the edges of the cut pane. The cuts were deep but uneven. They hadn't been made by any regular glass cutter; but they had been effective.

He went back into the main laboratory, picked up the telephone and called Thompson's number again.

"You might as well stay out of bed, chief," he said. "You won't get any sleep tonight. Ornstein has been bumped off now. Not a fire ball this time. Some one sneaked up and stabbed him with his own knife. You'll want to come over and take a look."

In fifteen minutes the siren of a fast police car made complaining echoes over the campus grounds. Wade had spent those fifteen minutes prowling around Ornstein's laboratory. But he hadn't found anything of interest. The still, marble-white face of the professor kept its secret. There was surprise rather than fear written on his dead features.

When Thompson arrived Wade told him all that he had seen and found, including the handkerchief with the initials Z. S. on it.

"It's Smith all right," said Thompson grimly. "But how to find him? He must have a hide-out somewhere near here."

The inspector turned and snapped orders to two of his men.

"Hunt around the campus. Look for his tracks. If you find one of his footprints near the fire escape we'll have him nailed as the murderer. Then we'll smoke him out of his hole if it takes a year."

He sent two other men on the run to Smith's dormitory.

"We've had the place shadowed," he said. "But he may have sneaked in."

All over the campus lights were springing up as the news of the murder spread to students and sleepy faculty members.

Wade began to examine the window again with Thompson at his side. Then the telephone in the outer laboratory began ringing harshly.

A detective picked it up, listened, then held the instrument out. There were tense lines in his face.

"Some one's calling for help!" he said.

Wade, stepping forward first, snatched the phone from the man's hand and put the receiver to his ear. A voice he recognized at once came over the wire.

"For God's sake—I'm being attacked—here in my laboratory—help—I—"

The voice trailed off in a wheezing gasp. It was Professor Hartz speaking.

Wade verified this from the frightened operator downstairs. Hartz had called the Institute switchboard and the operator had transferred the call to Ornstein's room, knowing the police were there.

"Come on," said Wade, turning to Thompson. "I know where Hartz is. Some one is up there with him—Doctor Zero, I think."

He went downstairs with Thompson and a detective at his side. They ran across a section of the campus and Wade led them to the building, on the top floor of which Hartz had his place.

Thompson fumed with impatience as the old-fashioned elevator in Hartz's building went skyward sluggishly.

"Hell," he said, "this place is like the Ark. He'll be dead by the time we get there."

But Hartz wasn't dead. A muffled voice called out in answer to their knock.

"Come in!"

HARTZ was on the floor, his head and shoulders resting against a couch. His collar and tie were ripped open. He was fingering his neck and gasping hoarsely. The room was in complete disorder with books and papers scattered around and a chair tipped over. The window was open. Hartz pointed toward it.

"He came through there—and left the same way." Hartz' voice was a hoarse croak. "I didn't see him. He grabbed me from behind."

Wade ran to the window. A fire escape zigzagged down here, too, and night shadows obscured its bottom.

Thompson lifted Hartz onto the sofa, then went and got him a drink of water from the cooler.

"Was it young Smith? Didn't you get a glimpse of him?"

Hartz shook his white head.

"No, but it was his hands I felt. The poor boy must have gone insane."

"Ornstein was murdered a few minutes ago," said Thompson. "We've got to locate Smith now. He and Doctor Zero are the same man."

Hartz nodded.

"An egomaniac," he said. "A man with a Napoleonic complex."

Wade recognized phrases from the terminology of popular psychology. He was staring around Hartz' laboratory. A skylight window lighted it in the daytime. Batteries of powerful bulbs hung down with silvered reflectors behind them to make the place bright at night. On three sides of the room the walls were lined with books and cabinets containing minerals and chemicals.

Wade seemed suddenly to loose interest in Hartz and what he was saying. He walked over to a book shelf and began taking down volumes. The professor turned his white head to stare at Wade's back. Inspector Thompson turned, too. His voice was sarcastic.

"We've got a murder investigation on our hands, Hammond. If you want to read why don't you join a library?"

But Wade wasn't reading. He couldn't seem to find a book that satisfied him. He was pulling them out now and piling them on a nearby table. Thompson spoke again.

"What the hell's the matter with you, Hammond? Have you gone nuts? Leave those books alone!"

Professor Hartz lifted his feet off the sofa and banged them down on the floor. His expression had suddenly changed.

"Keep away from my books," he snapped. "Leave them alone, young man."

Harsh' lines had come into the professor's face all at once. They were lines of poisonous bitterness; lines that seemed to have been etched there by hidden, unhealthy emotions and secret hell fires.

He rose and moved toward Wade, one clawlike hand stretched out and his eyes blazing. For Wade had paid no attention to either him or Thompson. He was pulling out more books and reaching in behind them.

Suddenly he grabbed two large red volumes. They left a hole in the shelf, and Wade's hand darted in. For a moment his fingers groped. Then there came a click of metal.

Wade stepped back and Inspector Thompson gasped. The shelves of books covering the whole side of the room were swinging outward, disclosing a door in the wall behind them.

"My God, Hammond—what's this?"

Thompson was staring in amazement at the secret door.

Professor Hartz seemed suddenly to have turned into a madman. He leaped toward Wade, his withered old features a hideous mask of hate. His eyes seemed inhuman in their ferocity. He wasn't the cool scientist now. His hands reached toward Wade's throat like talons. But Wade stepped aside and whirled. He gave Hartz a sudden violent push that sent him staggering back across the room.

"Watch him, chief. See that he doesn't pull a gun or a knife. I want to take a look in here."

WADE spoke with an air of confidence that left Thompson speechless. He pulled the hidden door open and stepped into the room behind it after snapping on a light switch. The room was another laboratory, compact and efficient, with a cement floor and a strange, squat piece of mechanism crouching in the center like an evil monster.

"Look!" Wade was pointing up toward the skylight.

There were windows up there which could be slid back on rollers, and, close to them, was the end of a telescoping metal shaft which had its base in the strange machine.

"I'm not enough of a scientist to tell you just what it is," said Wade. "But here's where those fire balls that killed Munn and the two detectives came from. It's an electro-atomic generator of some sort, capable of creating ball lightning which can be directed by means of a radio-active metal."

A noise interrupted his words. It was the sound of thumping feet. Some one was kicking on wood. It came from the door of a nearby closet. Wade walked over and flung it open. His face showed little surprise; but Thompson muttered in amazement.

Inside the closet a young man with a gag in his mouth was tied hand and foot and lying on the floor. He had drawn his knees up and was thumping his heels against the wall lustily. It was Zadok Smith.

Wade took a penknife from his pocket, reached down and freed the young man. Smith was willing to talk this time. Words tumbled over each other.

"What did that old buzzard mean—tying me up? Did Ornstein put him up to it—and what's this place here?"

"This," said Wade softly, "is Doctor Zero's laboratory. Our old friend, Hartz, has a dual personality. He's Doctor Zero, master criminal, with a brain fired by ambitious schemes, and Professor Hartz, Ph.D., savant of science. You've been studying with a versatile man, Smith. You should feel honored."

"Good God—you don't mean it! Hartz has been doing all this?"

"Yes, look over there, Smith. Even I can guess what he was doing here besides making lethal ball lightning. That was a side issue."

Wade was pointing toward one side of the secret laboratory. A big electric furnace stood on a metal table. There was a cooling tank beside it and a shelf of glass jars containing hundreds of carbon crystals.

"I knew he was bugs on the notion of making artificial diamonds," said Smith. "But I didn't guess he'd ever tried it."

"That was the motive behind his killings," said Wade. "He had to have money and lots of it for his experiments. It was why he thought of his extortion plot against Munn. He was nuts on diamonds. I felt when I first met him that those two stones he wore were somehow out of character. He even used a diamond to cut the glass on Ornstein's window. He must have thought Ornstein was getting suspicious and he went there to plant a chunk of metal as he did in my apartment and then send a couple of fire balls to do the trick. Ornstein caught him at it and Hartz used a knife to cover his tracks. He used you, Smith, to spy on Ornstein's electrical work and keep track of him."

Smith stammered and flushed.

"I thought Ornstein was the murderer," he said.

"Yes," said Wade. "You thought you were being a pretty clever amateur detective with that gadget of yours. I suppose you found that the fire balls came from the direction of the Institute."

"Yes, I thought Ornstein was sending them."

"So did I for a while," said Wade. "Hartz was clever. His acting just now showed that. He knew we'd suspect Ornstein and you. He dropped your handkerchief when he went to Ornstein's place to make sure."

T h o m p s o n edged forward. "There's one thing I don't get," he said. "Who kidnapped Miss Munn? Where is she?"

Wade nodded toward Smith. "I've got an idea you can answer that," he said.

Smith nodded and turned red again.

"I didn't kidnap her," he said. "I warned her that she was in danger and got her to hide for a while in a safe place. She was scared. She

didn't like Ornstein as much as she seemed to. She always trusted me. She's in a hotel in the country."

"That's another reason I began to think Smith wasn't the criminal," said Wade. "I figured by the tracks that Arlene Munn had left her aunt's willingly. Then that clue of the handkerchief in Ornstein's place was a little too obvious. That and the diamond scratches on the window made me think that Hartz was the murderer. With Ornstein dead and Smith out there seemed to be no one else. This room of Hartz' didn't look big enough to take up all the space here. I figured there was another room behind one of those book shelves."

Thompson wiped his face.

"You've done a swell job, Hammond. We may not land Hartz in the hot seat. They may send him to the bughouse instead. But with Doctor Zero out of the way we'll be able to get a good night's sleep again and the department will have some peace."

THE DEATH

As Lynn reached for the knob of the door, one of The Ghost's gunmen fired at him pointblank.

A
COMPLETE SHORT
G-77 NOVEL BY

BRYAN JAMES KELLEY

DEALER

A Gang That Shoots Its Way Through Steel Vaults Is The Newest
Menace Confronting The F.B.I. It's A Race Against Time As Lynn
Vickers And His G-Men Seek To End The Terror And Locate The
Source Of The New Invention That Threatens To Make One Man
A Ruthless Emperor Of The Underworld

CHAPTER I

The White-Faced Menace

LYNN VICKERS' lean, tanned face was grim and determined as he scanned the signs at a street corner in Chicago's South Side tenement district. If the tip-off the F. B. I. had received was on the level, Limpy Meslin was holed up in one of the dingy apartments along this street. The young G-man's wide shoulders squared and his jaw hardened at the thought. The end of the chase was drawing near.

For weeks the G-men had been trailing a ruthless gang of bank robbers that had been terrorizing the smaller cities of the middle-west; a new gang that had apparently sprung to life overnight. A gang that had struck a new and terrifying note in criminal ingenuity. Daylight hold-ups, blowing up vaults, all previous technique of bank robbers had been rendered obsolete by this fiendish mob. *For they had evolved a method of blasting their way through steel doors and vaults with bullets.*

VICKERS and his aides were completely baffled. The G-men did not know whether the new gang was using a new type gun or was in possession of a secret for making a deadly high explosive bullet that would penetrate highly tempered steel.

The possession of such a deadly weapon constituted a peril to the law forces of the country. The menace of the new, invincible weapon in the hands of gangland was being felt in an attitude of increased confidence in craven gangsters, in whisperings throughout the underworld of big crimes to come.

The harassed G-men had worked day and night, following the trail of the elusive gang of robbers. Apparently, so far, this gang had exclusive right to the new and terrible invention. And if the agents of the F. B. I. could get this gang, they would have the source of the new weapon before it was distributed throughout gangdom; they would prevent a crime wave such as the country had never experienced before.

And the Department of Justice had no idea as to the identity of the members of the new mob. Witnesses had told of a leader whose outstanding characteristic was the deadly pallor of his face. It was like the countenance of a dead man, expressionless, ghastly and immobile, they said. And in The Ghost, as the new criminal genius had been tabbed by the newspapers, Lynn Vickers grudgingly admitted he had met a foeman who threatened to overshadow any

criminal whom the ace sleuth of the F. B. I. had ever pursued.

Unceasing effort on the part of the G-men had narrowed down the field of activity until Vickers was certain that the headquarters of the new mob was located in Chicago. And now the finger had been put upon Limpy Meslin as a member of that mob, possibly as The Ghost himself.

As the tall, blond G-man swung down the narrow street, avoiding groups of half-naked children seeking relief from the sweltering heat of early evening on doorsteps and sidewalks, he mentally reviewed Meslin's criminal record.

Dark, stocky and handsome, Meslin had been one of the country's leading confidence men, operating as a lone wolf in rooking gullible farmers and widows of their life savings until he ran afoul of the law.

An accident in a prison stone quarry left him with a slight limp that gave him his nickname. He had emerged from prison embittered against the law forces that he blamed for his injury, and had earned a reputation for viciousness and daring that rated him as one of the country's leading public enemies.

Witnesses had twice identified a stocky, limping man as a member of the new mob of bank-robbers. The Ghost had not appeared in either of the jobs where Limpy was seen. Therefore, Vickers believed that Meslin might be The Ghost, working sometimes in disguise and at other times without, to baffle and confuse the police and G-men.

Ruthless and desperate, Limpy Meslin wouldn't be taken without a fight.

G-77 hoped he could take Meslin alive. Possession of the secret of the sinister new weapon used by the mob was as important as the capture of The Ghost himself. And the next thirty minutes might see the accomplishment of both tasks. His lean, tanned face bleak, Lynn Vickers was transformed from a quiet, pleasant-looking young man into a grim, alert man-hunter about to face one of the most dangerous jobs in his career as a G-man.

Half-way down the block, G-77 was suddenly frozen in his tracks by a loud, piercing scream. It was a cry laden with fear and it caused Vickers' eyes to jerk upward just in time to see a writhing, spinning body hurtling down from the roof of an apartment house. And before he could move the body had dropped with a sickening thud at his feet.

Hair lifted at the back of Lynn Vickers' neck as he jumped to one side. He glimpsed a white face framed by long, unkempt hair. Terror had twisted the falling man's facial muscles into a dreadful mask. Skinny hands were frozen into claws in a frenzy of horror and despair.

LYNN VICKERS

The man had landed on his back on the sidewalk. The shock had shattered all the bones in his body; his limbs were limp and twisted like those of a rag doll. Blood poured from his ears, mouth and nostrils.

Women in house dresses and men in shirtsleeves gathered quickly around the mangled body. Children edged furtively through the crowd, gaping in horror. A patrolman pounded up the sidewalk, elbowed through and drove the avid spectators back. A prowl car siren shrieked as its driver raced toward the spot.

VICKERS stood by the curb, his eyes on the crumpled cadaver. The man was well past middle age, dressed in shabby clothes that had once been well-tailored. Refinement and intelligence showed in his seamed face, wide-spaced eyes, the high, sloping forehead and the firm, cleft chin that was gray with a stubble of beard where it wasn't crimson with blood.

The patrolman mopped his brow,

glanced toward the apartment house roof and muttered, "Poor devil! The heat must have gotten him."

"That man wasn't a suicide," Vickers said sharply. "Look at his feet."

The cop shot a quick glance at the G-man. Then his eyes slithered to the dead man's feet. They were bare and the soles were a charred mass of raw flesh matted with tar and gravel!

G-77 said tersely, "He's been tortured. He either ran or was chased across the roof to plunge to his death. That man was murdered!"

The patrolman looked up. "Say, who in hell are you?" he asked sharply.

Vickers did some fast thinking. He did not wish to reveal his identity. Friends of Limpy Meslin might be in the throng that crowded the narrow street, and tip the gangster off that the Federals were closing in on him. But the atrocity of the murder of the gray-haired old man fanned the hatred the young agent had for all criminals into flames of anger. He wanted to see the fiend who had committed this crime brought to justice. Vickers flashed his identification papers, then swore under his breath as the policeman blurted aloud:

"Lynn Vickers! My name's Hurley, sir. I'm glad to know you."

Whispers spread through the crowd as the name of the famous Federal agent went from mouth to mouth.

Then Vickers saw two men from the prowl car shove through the crowd. One was a uniformed policeman, the other a plainclothes detective.

Hurley introduced the plainclothes man as Detective Jaffee. The city detective rapped quick orders, then started into the lobby of the apartment house with Vickers. The self-service elevator was just coming down as they entered.

Before they reached the door it shot back up again.

"That may be the killer. We blocked his escape. He's heading back up. Let's take the stairs and cover each floor."

It was the G-man who spoke and he was in action before he finished. Breath was hammering in his lungs when they reached the top floor of the ten-story building. Jaffee was red-faced and puffing. They had checked the closets and fire-escape landings on each floor, making sure the killer had not doubled back.

In the tenth floor hall Vickers stopped suddenly, pointing to dark brown smears leading from the apartment nearest the stairs to the roof.

"There's the tracks of the dead man's bleeding feet," he grated. Jaffee swore. Then they raced up the stairs. The detective stopped G-77 for a second at the landing.

"Let me go first," Jaffee said. "I'm wearing a bullet-proof vest."

But Vickers shook his head, lifted his gun from its clip holster, twisted the knob, crouched and hit the door with his shoulder. His wary eyes raked every shadow as he plunged out, Jaffee at his side. The roof was still and quiet. Hugging the shadows of the coping, they circled in opposite directions, making sure that the killer was not lurking in the shadows of the elevator shaft or the structure that housed the stairwell.

Jaffee supplemented the faint light from the stars and street lamps with the beam of a pocket flash. They followed the trail of bloody footprints across the roof to the three-foot parapet.

"The old man was chased up here," grated Vickers. "He didn't have a chance to hide. The killer must have been right at his heels." His eyes scanned the roof. "The building in back is a little lower than this one. There's only a narrow alley between them. The killer could have made a getaway there."

THE detective started to shift his flashlight beam to the next roof but Vickers said, "Just a minute, Jaffee. I want to look at this mud." Jaffee's flash picked up a small clump of reddish mud on the edge of the parapet. The G-man scraped it up, carefully put it into an envelope and tucked it into his inside pocket.

"Somebody carried that mud up here," he explained to Jaffee. "It was dropped recently or this heat would have pulverized it. Look, there's another lump."

Jaffee moved closer as Vickers bent to retrieve the second clump. The G-man was about to reach for the mud when a sharp *ping* and a grunt from Jaffee stopped his hand in mid-air.

He whirled to see the detective, a look of bewildered amazement on his face, clutching his shirt over his heart. Vickers leaped to his feet as Jaffee staggered toward the parapet, blood seeping through his fingers.

G-77 made a desperate leap toward the falling man. Cloth slipped through Vickers' fingers as the plainclothes man's two hundred pounds balanced for a split second on the round, smooth tile of the coping and then slid down into the dark void of the alley.

Startled, electrifying thoughts flashed through Vickers' brain, as he saw Jaffee's body hurtling toward the pavement. The plainclothes man had been wearing a steel bullet-proof vest, yet the assassin's bullet had pierced the chilled metal links like so much cheese! That would mean but one thing. The killer must be a member of The Ghost's mob! Maybe it was the phantom leader himself!

The significance of this startling development galvanized G-77 into action. He wanted to examine Jaffee's riddled vest. As he straightened a hot, searing pain lanced his shoulder. Lynn dropped quickly below the parapet. The killer was still on the next roof!

Another bullet sheared through the tile just over his head. He raced along the roof screened by the parapet. At the doorway leading to the stairs he straightened, his eyes r a k i n g the shadows of the roof below. A black blob moved down there. His automatic roared twice. He ducked again as a stab of orange and blue pierced the murk on the other roof. The whine of the bullet flicked past his head.

The G-man swore viciously. He couldn't return the fire without exposing himself, and if he tried to leap to the next roof, he would be picked off in mid-air.

Then the door leading onto the roof crashed open. A big man in civilian clothes plunged out. Vickers recognized Lieutenant Leyhan of the Homicide Division, an officer with whom he had worked before.

"Look out, Leyhan," Vickers yelled. "The killer is on the next roof!"

Simultaneously a bullet smacked into the stucco beside Leyhan's head. Leyhan ducked around the corner of the structure. Vickers raced for the shelter of the same stair-well housing.

Leyhan sputtered profanely, spitting out bits of tobacco. "How did he get Jaffee? He usually wears a steel vest," he panted. Vickers explained briefly. The big lieutenant swore. "One of The Ghost's mob, eh? We can't let that rat get away."

"There may be a chance if both of us jump to the next roof in different spots," Vickers said grimly. "He's using a silenced gun. That means he can only fire single shots. One of us might make it."

They separated about twenty feet apart as they raced for the parapet. Vickers' heart did a flip-flop as he sprang for the top of the coping. If his foot slipped on the smooth tile he would hurtle down ten stories to crash on the pavement below.

Then he hit the top of the parapet and launched out into space. His nerves tensed as the other roof rushed up to meet him. Each second he ex-

pected to feel the impact of a bullet from the deadly weapon in the hands of the murderer.

He landed on his hands and knees. He heard Leyhan hit the roof a second later. Soon the big lieutenant was beside him, and they crouched there, getting their breath and their bearings.

Then they separated and started a furtive search of the roof, automatics in hand, ears attuned for the slightest sound. They circled the roof and met at the stair well. Vickers tried the door leading to the stairs and found it locked.

Whirling abruptly, he raced to the steel skeleton of the fire-escape and swore as he glimpsed a dark figure near the bottom platform. He blazed two shots down, and heard them ricochet off the steel grilled steps as the killer slid from sight over the edge of the fire-escape into the shadows below.

CHAPTER II

Vickers Springs a Trap

VICKERS and Leyhan lost no further time in getting to the street. G-77 was convinced now that the murder of the old man was definitely tied up with The Ghost and his mob. But what was the connection? Was the man who escaped Limpy Meslin? Vickers determined to settle that point at once. Limpy's hideout was only a few doors further down the street.

He outlined his theory to Leyhan in clipped sentences, then pushed his way through the crowd and hurried along the sidewalk to the address furnished by the stool pigeon who had put the finger on Limpy.

But his quest was futile. The superintendent of the building told him that a man answering Meslin's description had lived there for a month, but had left the day before, leaving no forwarding address. Vickers cursed under his breath as he went back to join Leyhan. He had come to the end of another blind trail, like the ones they had followed for weeks.

The medical examiner's assistant had completed his task when G-77 rejoined Leyhan. There was no bullet wound on the old man. Fear or pain had made him take the suicidal leap from the roof.

Mrs. Flynn, the lean, slatternly owner of the apartment house, had identified the victim as Warren Chesley, a cracked inventor who had occupied a cheap apartment on the top floor. His place was always cluttered up with crazy inventions, she said, but he was a nice, kindly old soul who wouldn't harm a fly.

AT the mention of inventions, Lynn Vickers became alert. Could this white-haired old crack-pot have fathered the diabolical implement that had made The Ghost and his mob a deadly menace? A glance at the seamed, refined face in the wicker basket the internes were lifting killed the thought. Warren Chesley did not look like the sort of man who would be dealing with murderers and bandits.

A commotion at the edge of the crowd focused G-77's attention on a stocky, well-dressed, round-faced man who was crowding toward the basket. Vickers saw the man's pink cheeks pale, heard him catch his breath sharply. Bright blue eyes that glinted with horror and amazement turned to Vickers. The man gasped:

"What happened to Chesley, officer? Has there been an accident?"

Leyhan's cold eye took in the compact figure, from the expensive panama down to the oxfords of fine cordovan. He snapped, "Who are you?"

"My name is Steele—Guy Steele," the pink-cheeked man said. His tones were slightly pompous as he fished an engraved card from a case and handed it to Leyhan. "I'm a broker. Chesley is an old friend of mine. His daughter and son-in-law, Kirk Mabie, are neighbors of mine out on North Shore Drive. Splendid old gentleman, but a little bit peculiar on his hobby of inventions. He

called me today, all excited about some big discovery, wanted me to look it over. That's why I came here tonight. Never thought I'd find him—dead. Was it an accident?"

"It was murder," Leyhan clipped.

Vickers saw Steele's cheeks turn gray, and his blue eyes opened wide.

"Murder?" he said in shocked tones. "Why would anyone want to murder poor old Warren Chesley?"

"That's what we want to know."

Vickers had been sizing the broker up keenly. The man seemed to be genuinely shocked and grieved. The young G-man asked quietly, "Did you ever hear Chesley mention any contacts with the underworld, Mr. Steele? Or any personal enemies?"

Guy Steele's round face was a picture of surprise and shocked protest.

"Heavens, no!" he exclaimed. "Warren Chesley wouldn't know a crook or a gangster if he saw one."

"That may be the answer," Vickers muttered cryptically.

He then questioned the landlady about visitors Chesley might have had. She mentioned a lovely blonde woman, expensively dressed, who came nearly every week. Guy Steele interrupted to explain that the woman would be the old inventor's daughter, Mrs. Arlene Chesley Mabie. When Vickers asked why the wealthy daughter permitted her father to live in such sordid surroundings, Steele looked embarrassed, muttered something about family quarrels and said he'd rather let Mrs. Mabie answer that question herself.

When the internes took the body away, Vickers and Leyhan started up to Chesley's apartment. Steele seemed offended when Vickers curtly refused him permission to accompany them. G-77's eyes were speculative as he watched the nattily dressed broker distastefully elbowing his way back through the crowd.

Just as they were entering the apartment house, the landlady said, "I almost forgot to tell you about another feller that came here a couple times to see Mr. Chesley. He was a dark, good-looking man, kind of lame. He was here a couple times. Last night he came but the old gentleman was out. The lame man seemed pretty mad because he couldn't find him."

Vickers tensed at her words. The description tallied with that of Limpy Meslin! This was positive proof that in some mysterious way, Warren Chesley was hooked up with The Ghost and his mob.

THE apartment on the tenth floor looked as if a hurricane had hit it. A table that had been used as a work-bench was up-ended, tools, bits of wood and steel were scattered about the floor. A cheap day-bed had been torn apart, its thin mattress ripped to shreds. A shabby cogswell chair was tipped over and a Bunsen burner stood on the floor in front of the chair.

Vickers felt the burner. It was still hot. He saw some strips of cotton beneath the overturned chair and his face hardened at the significance of what he saw. He pointed this out to Leyhan.

"Chesley was tied in the chair. The torturer worked on his feet with the Bunsen burner. Chesley must have passed out or got knocked out when the chair tipped over. They searched the room while Chesley was unconscious. The old man must have worked loose and made a wild break for freedom— that ended down there on the sidewalk."

Leyhan agreed. "I wonder what the rats were looking for? Maybe Chesley had some invention even worse than this damned mystery weapon the mob is using."

The homicide men picked up several sets of prints. They also gathered up blueprints and working models of inventions. Laboratory men at headquarters would check them in hopes that they might reveal the secret of Warren Chesley's atrocious murder.

Underworld haunts were scoured for Limpy Meslin, but the swarthy, handsome desperado had vanished into thin air.

Laboratory scientists reported on the red clay Vickers had found on the roof. The only similar deposit around Chicago was located in the swanky North Shore district.

Vickers went with Leyhan to question the daughter of the murdered inventor.

Mrs. Mabie, a slender, beautiful woman in her early thirties, was deeply shocked and grieved by her father's terrible death. Anguish and self-condemnation shook her voice as she explained why her father did not live with her. Kirk Mabie, her husband, had offered Chesley a position in the big engraving and printing plant he owned in Ravenswood, but the dead man had not liked his son-in-law. He had bitterly resented Mabie's jeers at his inventions. Her father had a small income and had preferred living alone where he could putter with his brain creations.

He had, however, spent most of his week-ends at his daughter's home in the North Shore district.

Arlene Mabie could throw no light on the atrocious murder. Her father never talked about his inventions, perhaps because of Mabie's rough sarcasm. During his week-end visits he spent most of his time in an old abandoned cemetery near their home, where he would spend hour after hour alone. He hadn't an enemy in the world, so far as she knew.

"Not much help there," Leyhan said glumly, after they had left. Vickers frowned and ran his fingers through his blond hair.

"That cemetery angle interests me," he said thoughtfully. "Chesley didn't look like a morbid bird who would hang around graveyards for no good reason. I want to see that cemetery. I'd like to see if that red clay belt runs through it. I want to have a talk with Kirk Mabie, too. I've got a hunch there's more to the ill-feeling between him and Chesley than we figure. His wife acted nervous when she told you about it."

Leyhan returned to headquarters but an hour later G-77 was at the Mabie Engraving plant. Kirk Mabie was a dark, swarthy-skinned man, with hair starting to thin at the top. His brown eyes were set close together and they avoided Vickers' gaze, shifting uneasily while he answered the G-man's questions. He seemed to feel badly about his father-in-law's death. Almost too badly, Vickers thought cynically. When questioned about Chesley's inventions, Mabie shrugged his heavy shoulders and said, "The old man was cracked on that subject; always on the verge of making a million. He wasted a comfortable fortune on his crazy ideas."

"A fortune that his daughter would have inherited?" Vickers asked softly.

"That's right," Mabie snapped. Then his dark face flushed and his stocky figure stiffened. "Say," he growled, "you aren't insinuating anything, are you?"

"Hell, no," Vickers said easily. But Mabie's peculiar expression had registered. "Have you any idea what Chesley might have invented that a mob of killers would want badly enough to murder him for it?"

Mabie hesitated a second. Then he shook his head and said, "It's beyond me, Mr. Vickers. He was not the sort of man who would have had dealings with crooks. In fact, he used to say that some day he hoped to give the government an invention that would help to exterminate all the rats in the underworld. It was just wild raving, of course, but it shows what his feelings were toward gangsters."

Mabie was unable to throw any light on Chesley's strange visits to the cemetery. As Vickers was leaving, he asked suddenly, "Do you happen to know Guy Steele?"

Mabie gave a quick start, then laughed nervously as he said, "Sure, everybody knows Steele. He's the city's outstanding playboy. What's he got to do with the case?"

"Was he friendly with your father-in-law?"

"He got a kick out of the old man's wild ideas. He used to say Chesley was like a character out of a book."

LEYHAN'S brow was furrowed with worry when G-77 walked into his office an hour or so later. He had returned, after leaving Vickers, to find his office in an uproar over the reported disappearance of Seth Worden, a millionaire inventor and manufacturer. Leyhan had investigated immediately and learned that Worden had started for his office the previous morning, but had never arrived there. No word had been received from him. Neither his family nor business associates could account for his disappearance.

"Hell," Leyhan growled profanely. "It must be open season on inventors. Do you suppose The Ghost put the snatch on Worden?"

"It wouldn't surprise me," Vickers said morosely. "We're bucking a damned clever gang. I rate The Ghost as one of the most dangerous criminals at large today. There's no limit to the scope of his crimes. The success of his mob has influenced the underworld and is breeding a bold contempt of the law. We've got to stop The Ghost or we'll have a crime wave on our hands that can never be halted."

"You still figure Limpy Meslin is the big shot of the mob?"

"Meslin is a brainy, ruthless devil. If he isn't at the head of the mob, he's certainly very near the top. Once we get our hands on him, we're well on our way to wiping out The Ghost."

"By God, we'll find him," Leyhan swore wrathfully. "I'll start a dragnet that will cover every hideout and rathole in the city."

IT was one of Vickers' agents, however, who located the lame fugitive in a cheap boarding house on the West Side. Dan Hillary, the special agent in charge of the Chicago office, suggested surrounding the house and closing in on Meslin. But G-77 was afraid that a raid might put Limpy to flight. Mulcher, who was Limpy's landlord, had been suspected of harboring crooks before. Undoubtedly he had arranged some means of escape for his "wanted" tenants in case of a visit from the law. Vickers believed that he would be more successful single-handed.

A few minutes later the blond agent was headed for the West Side in a district car. Vickers was so preoccupied with mapping out his plan of attack that he failed to notice the disreputable coupé that trailed him across the bridge, following him until he was within three blocks of Meslin's hideout.

Vickers parked his car a half block from the hideout, swung back and circled around the block, scanning the three-story frame house. Shabby awnings covered most of the windows on the west side. The grimy building looked deserted, sweltering in the afternoon heat.

The G-man rounded the corner,

turned sharply and swung into the narrow vestibule. His right hand fastened around the butt of the automatic in his pocket as he jabbed the bell. A minute later a fat, perspiring, bald-headed man opened the door, peering at G-77 through thick-lensed glasses.

"Mr. Mulcher?' Vickers asked briskly, crowding into the dingy hall. The man nodded slowly, suspicion and apprehension clouded his pale blue eyes.

"Uh-huh," he grunted. "What you want?"

"I want Limpy Meslin," Vickers clipped. "I'm a Federal agent. We know Meslin is hiding out here, so don't stall. And don't try any funny business or you'll get yours for harboring a public enemy. Take me to Meslin's room—and be quiet about it."

Mulcher's eyes darted toward the stairs, he started to shake his head, but the steely glint of the G-man's eye changed his mind. He wet his thick lips and said huskily, "I don't know if he's in or not."

"Show me his room," Vickers growled. He emphasized the command with a movement of the gun in his pocket.

Mulcher started up the stairs with Vickers at his heels. At the top landing he pointed to a door.

"The second room. But please, mister, don't say I put the finger on him. I'd get rubbed out for it, sure."

"Okay," Vickers nodded. "Beat it downstairs—and stay there."

CAUTIOUSLY Vickers approached the door to Meslin's room. The palm that gripped his gun was sweaty. Fervently he prayed that Limpy Meslin would be in, that success would at last crown his weeks of futile effort.

He listened for a second for any sound from within the room. His fingers twisted the door knob, the automatic jerked from his pocket and his shoulder hit the door.

The G-man's eyes lighted on a figure stretched prone on the bed that came up with a jerk, clawed under the pillow for a gun, thought better of it when he saw G-77's pistol, and raised his hands above his head. Vickers got a good look at him then and knew it wasn't Limpy Meslin.

The man's frantic move for his gun had betrayed him as a fugitive from justice, however. Vickers' brain clicked fast. Limpy must have a roommate. The thin-faced hoodlum was probably a member of The Ghost's mob. The G-man's automatic lined on the hood.

"Don't try it, mug, unless you're asking for sudden death," he said.

The man's hands came into view. He snarled, "Okay, you're in the driver's seat. What's the big idea? You ain't got anything on me."

Vickers' face was grim and menacing. "We've only got three bank robberies and a couple of killings on you, mug. You're going to take the rap for The Ghost. Grab your hat and come along."

The thug's sallow face went livid with fear. Vickers' voice carried conviction. He started to squawk frantically.

"You can't get away with a frame like that!" he yelled. "I don't know anything about the The Ghost."

"Save it for the jury," clipped Vickers. "When Leyhan and his strong-arm squad get through with you, perhaps your memory will be better. The boys at headquarters took Detective Jaffee's murder rather hard. They won't be very gentle with you."

"Don't turn me over to the cops!" the hoodlum cried. "They'll murder me! Give me a chance, will you?"

Elation filled Vickers' heart. The cowardly crook was cracking. He said crisply, "I'll give you a break. Answer a couple of questions and I'll book you as a material witness and guarantee your safety."

The man nodded eagerly.

"Who is The Ghost?" snapped Vickers.

"I don't know, but I think Chesley's son-in-law is the big shot. I heard Limpy say he kicked in with—"

A brittle, muffled voice from the hall brought Vickers about like a flash. "You lousy rat! Ready to spill your guts, are you?"

Vickers' eyes whirled to the stocky, dark-clad figure in the door. Bitterness numbed the G-man's brain as he stared at the corpse-like face of the man who cradled a long-barreled rifle in the hollow of his arm. For a split second Vickers' desperate glance flicked to a second man who had crowded through the doorway. Then his eyes came back to the man who had spoken.

He was dressed in black—hat, suit, shoes—even his hands were encased in black gloves. Against this somber background the man's face was startlingly white — bloodless and ghastly. The effect was shocking, until Vickers saw that he wore a white rubber mask that fitted his features closely, completely hiding them. Dark eyes blazed through the slits of the mask. The muffled voice said, "Drop that rod, Vickers, or the tommy-gun starts talking."

Despair that was like physical illness swept over Lynn Vickers. He was face to face with The Ghost—the man who was responsible for the murder of Chesley and Jaffee. He had found the master-mind of the bank-robbing mob—only to meet death at the hands of the evil genius of crime.

CHAPTER III
The Devil's Genius

"SO you walked into my trap," sneered The Ghost. "I figured on a rumor that Limpy Meslin was here being good bait. I've had an idea that this rat on the bed had the makings of a squealer, that's why I had him here to keep you occupied until I could get here."

Vickers' brain was racing. The man on the bed screamed a shrill denial that he was going to squeal.

The Ghost ignored him, spoke to the man beside him who held a tommy-gun in his hands.

"You take the squealer. I'll take care of the famous Mister Vickers."

The muzzle of the sub-machine gun shifted, and Lynn Vickers made his desperate play for freedom in the same split second. His hand whipped up and his automatic snarled. He saw The Ghost's movement to bring the rifle up halted as the slug rapped against his chest, staggering him. Then the mouth of the rubber mask peeled back in a ferocious grin. And Vickers knew that the masked leader was wearing a steel vest.

In the split second it took the gang leader to regain his balance, Vickers whirled and leaped straight for the window looking out to the street on the west side.

Behind him the tommy-gun chattered and a scream from the man on the bed ended sharply. Shielding his face with his arms, Vickers smashed through flying glass. A hot flash branded his scalp and he knew The Ghost's bullet had grazed him.

Then his hands flew out, clutching at the steel frame of the awning that shaded the window. He swung pen-dulum fashion twice, then dropped just as bullets from the tommy-gun ripped through the canvas over his head.

He plummeted down, striving tensely to hit the awning of the window directly beneath. The sidewalk rushed up to meet him at a sickening rate of speed. His feet hit the canvas. It ripped with a sharp, explosive sound and he shot through the tattered shreds. Hands extended, he grasped at the framework. His arms were nearly jerked from their socket, but he managed to retain his grip long enough to break the force of his fall. His body was bathed with cold sweat when he dropped to the sidewalk and raced around the corner.

A prowl car siren sounded down the street. The fusillade of shots had brought police help, but it would arrive too late. G-77 knew that even now The Ghost and his chopper would be making a getaway.

Sick with disappointment, Vickers made a search of the house with the officers of the prowl car. Mulcher had disappeared. So had The Ghost and the torpedo. An open back door marked the path of their flight. The criminal genius had played him for a sucker, trapped him, damned near murdered him and escaped. Disheartening doubt bogged Lynn Vickers' brain as he climbed in his car and started back to F. B. I. headquarters to have his scalp patched. The only thing he had to work on now was the remark the dead squealer had made about Chesley's son-in-law.

VICKERS was hollow-eyed and jittery when he visited Lieut. Leyhan at police headquarters next day. Long hours of ceaseless effort had failed to uncover any further trace of Limpy Meslin. G-77 had asked for a close check on Kirk Mabie, but the report was not completed. However, he did have another significant new lead.

Chesley's landlady had identified a picture of Seth Worden, the missing millionaire inventor, as a frequent visitor at Chesley's apartment and added that she'd often heard the two men quarreling.

"Our agents have been checking on Worden," Vickers said. "His reputation is pretty sour. He's pirated a lot of inventions, had a couple of law suits over infringements of patents and is reputed to have grabbed off inventions of his employees. Worden sizes up as a mean old devil greedy for money and not particular how he gets it."

Leyhan looked thoughtful, chewed on a cigar and growled, "I believe you're right. Worden wasn't kidnaped or there would have been a demand for ransom before this. He may have tried to buy some invention of Chesley's, failed, and took other means of getting it. If he's The Ghost he wouldn't stop at murder."

"He certainly lines up with Mabie and Limpy as suspects," G-77 agreed. "Though after yesterday's experience Kirk Mabie rates number one on my list. That thug wasn't stalling when he put the finger on Chesley's son-in-law. I grilled Mabie last night and he couldn't give me an alibi for yesterday afternoon. He was out of his office during the time The Ghost was trying to gun me out."

"What do you make of this mugg Steele?" asked Leyhan. "He's getting in my hair. Called up four times to know what progress has been made in Chesley's murder hunt, and today he got tough and threatened to use his political drag to have someone hauled over the coals unless something is done pretty quick."

"We've got to expect that," Vickers said wearily. "The papers are beginning to ride us too. Steele seems to be on the up-and-up. However, I've put Tommy Dewart, an agent who's been with me on some of my toughest cases, and a girl named Evelyn March—one of the smartest undercover operatives in the F. B. I.—on both Mabie's and Steele's tails. They both have a weakness for skirts. Miss March is working on that angle, trying to contact some of their women friends."

Lynn Vickers' haggard face softened and his eyes brightened as he spoke of Evelyn March. He had never told the lovely, auburn-haired beauty about his love for her because he was pledged to a career of man-hunting, inspired by a deep hatred of criminals since the day that his father—duped by a ruthless political swindler who had double-crossed the senior Vickers and left him holding the bag—had committed suicide rather than face disgrace and a long prison sentence for a crime of which he was innocent. It was then that Lynn Vickers had deserted a profitable law practice to join the F. B. I. and devote his life to hunting criminals. He had achieved success in his chosen field. G-77 was feared and hated in the underworld of two continents. And because of this success he always walked in paths of danger. Therefore love had no place in the life of Lynn Vickers, ace-sleuth of the F. B. I.

A strip of adhesive tape made a livid streak along G-77's blond head. The bandages around his ribs covering another wound from the Death Dealer's rifle felt like a corset. Vickers felt like a battle-scarred veteran as he went to meet Tommy after leaving Leyhan's office.

At the hotel, Lynn briefly outlined his plans to the lanky G-man. Evelyn would try to contact Kirk Mabie in one of the swanky night clubs that he frequented. At the same time, she would try to get a line on Guy Steele, who traveled with the same crowd. He and Tommy would concentrate on Limpy Meslin and Seth Worden.

Tommy Dewart listened eagerly as G-77 outlined his theory. The Ghost was already in possession of one deadly device. Armed with guns that would drive bullets through steel, the Death Dealer and his mob were almost invincible. But the murder of Warren Chesley pointed to the possibility of another secret—another invention that would be a further menace to the agents of the law. Every hour, now, that The Ghost remained free made the chances of his capture more remote. If Vickers' theory was correct, the murderous mob could never be stopped once they had the new death weapon operating.

"Where do we start?" Tommy asked cheerfully when Lynn had finished talking.

"I want to take a look at that cemetery near Mabie's house," G-77 replied. "Chesley used to spend a lot of time there. There may be a clue there."

They drove out to the cemetery that

mering at walls, stamping on floors. Cobwebs and dust grimed their faces. They were ready to admit their task was hopeless, when Tommy called excitedly to Vickers.

"The hinges on this vault have been oiled, Lynn. There's footprints of red clay around the sill."

"Get your hands up!" Vickers said. "One false move and somebody heads for hell." (Page 28)

covered the long, sloping hill a few hundred yards from Kirk Mabie's big English Colonial house in the North Shore colony.

Prowling among the sagging tombstones, they devoted most of their attention to the ancient mausoleums that dotted the hillside. Most of them were overgrown with weeds and shrubbery.

Daylight faded into dusk as they explored nearly a dozen sepulchres, ham-

Vickers' heart skipped a beat as he came over to pull open the door. But as he reached for it, a *spinging* noise caused him to duck instinctively. And before his startled eyes a round hole showed in the heavy iron door!

He whirled on the balls of his feet. Tommy had ducked, too, and then both ducked for the bushes that surrounded the mausoleum.

"It's The Ghost—that was a steel-blasting gun!" Vickers said tersely.

Tommy nodded. "What do we do—"

The roar of a motor cut through his speech. Tommy grated a curse, as he listened to the grinding gears of a departing car. "What in hell does that signify?" he asked. "A warning that we aren't wanted in this graveyard?"

Vickers looked thoughtful. "Maybe," he said. "But it also means that every move we make is being watched. It's just a little example of the diabolical genius we're up against, Tommy."

CHAPTER IV

In the Cemetery

THEIR faces were sober as they went back to the gloomy vault. G-77 felt that they would learn nothing there. If they had been on the trail of anything hot, The Ghost would not have left them there.

They found a spot where someone had been digging, but after scooping out the soft dirt they discovered only that the wall of the tomb was cracked and a piece had been broken out. The tunnel ended abruptly at the broken wall. Dirt caved in from the outside, opening a passageway under the vault wall. But that was all, and it didn't seem to have any significance.

"It looks like a blind trail, Tommy," G-77 said finally. "Someone started to tunnel here, then gave it up as a bad job. It's too dark to do any more exploring. We'll have to come back. I still feel there's something here. The Ghost's leaving us here after firing that shot would indicate he merely came to show us he knows our every move. But it could also be a clever ruse to steer us away from this cemetery."

From the cemetery the two G-men went directly to the Mabie mansion, which was within sight of the eerie spot. Kirk Mabie answered their ring. His dark face flushed angrily as he recognized Vickers.

"Well, what is it now, Mastermind?" he snapped. "Thought up some more questions for me to answer?"

"I just wanted to know whether you could handle a rifle," G-77 said quietly.

Mabie's stocky figure stiffened. His dark brown eyes glinted dangerously.

"I was captain of the rifle team at the military school I attended," he rapped viciously. "So what does that make me?"

"It might make you the killer that just took a shot at us up in the cemetery," Vickers said.

Mabie took a short step toward the G-men, his big hands knotted into fists and his voice hoarse with suppressed fury.

"You accuse me of trying to shoot you? Trying to frame me as the goat, are you? By God, I'll make you sweat for this persecution. I know my rights as a citizen, and I've got money enough to fight for them."

Tommy edged closer. But Vickers remained unruffled, as he said, "It's a good act, Mabie, but I've a hunch The Ghost is no stranger to you. And I'm not stepping out until I know where you stand."

Mabie looked as if he were on the verge of an apoplectic stroke, as he slammed the door behind Vickers and Tommy.

In the car Tommy said, "You've got him badly worried, Lynn. Do you think he is The Ghost?"

"I don't know," G-77 admitted. "If he is he knows we suspect him. It may rattle him into making a careless move. That's the best we can hope for now."

The F. B. I. office was buzzing with excitement the next morning. A bank in Evanston had been robbed during the night and a cashier and watchman killed. The bank stayed open on Friday nights from 7:00 to 9:00 P.M. The holdup took place just at the closing hour.

Witnesses differed in their descriptions of the thugs who had done the killing. But on one point all witnesses agreed. Two men had been in the rear seat of the bandits' car, and one of them was The Ghost! There could be no mistaking the descriptions of the white, ghastly face.

Lynn Vickers swore viciously when he heard the story. "Find out where Kirk Mabie was at nine o'clock last night. Unless he has an iron-clad alibi, bring him in. I'll take a chance on his raising hell for a false arrest."

Evelyn March reported on the result of her check-up on Guy Steele the night before. The broker had entertained a platinum blonde at the Club Madrid until two in the morning. He left the girl at her hotel about two-twenty and then proceeded to his home on North Shore Drive.

"Guess that eliminates Steele as a suspect," Vickers said flatly.

"Maybe it does on last night's job," Evelyn said excitedly. "But I've got a hunch that Guy Steele hooks into this case somewhere. The girl he entertained was Sara Nova, who used to be an entertainer at Ballsimo's club, the hangout for all the big-shot racketeers in the city. Allan Goff, the local agent who acted as my escort, tabbed her for me. And Goff tells me that the platinum-haired, sloe-eyed Sara used to be Limpy Meslin's sweetheart—and may still be."

Vickers whistled under his breath. He said slowly, "Steele would make an ideal 'fence' for the hot bonds and securities the mob picks up at the banks. The girl may be acting as a go-between. You'll have to tail her, Red Head."

"How about Steele?" Evelyn asked. "He gave me the glad eye once or twice last night. Maybe I can chisel in on the Nova dame's time."

"I think the girl offers a better lead. She might put us on Limpy Meslin's trail. I'll have Steele shadowed, too. But you stick to the Nova girl."

A PHONE call a few minutes later gave Kirk Mabie an alibi during the time of the holdup. The agent who was sent to check on Mabie reported that he and his wife were having dinner at the Palmer House at nine o'clock. They stayed until after ten P.M.

Steele and Mabie had iron-clad alibis. That narrowed the list of suspects down to Limpy Meslin and Seth Worden. And both of these men had completely disappeared from sight. G-77 knew the latest crime would bring a storm of protest down on their heads. Washington would be demanding explanations. The Ghost had scored another coup.

"The Evanston Bank was a Federal Reserve depository," he growled. "That drops it square in our laps, Tommy. You'd better go out there and take charge. And for God's sake, don't pass up anything that will offer the faintest clue toward identifying this devil who is making monkeys out of us."

Through the assistance of Dan Hillary, Vickers got Evelyn placed as a Western Union clerk in the lobby of the hotel where Sara Nova was living. From that vantage point the red head could keep tabs on the platinum-haired entertainer.

Vickers went down to headquarters, checked with Lieutenant Leyhan on any new developments. The big Irishman shook his head dolefully. There was still no trace of Limpy Meslin.

They discussed the Evanston robbery, and when Vickers told of the alibis that had been established for Mabie and Steele, Leyhan said vehemently:

"We've been trailing the wrong dogs, Vickers. Worden is the man we want. I think he's the inventor of the new gun they're using to blast into those banks."

"Worden does fit the picture very well," Vickers said reluctantly. "Your men haven't picked up his trail, have they?"

Leyhan growled deep in his throat. A black scowl marred his forehead as he clipped, "We could have had our hands on him early this morning if a dumb-bell I had watching his house hadn't been asleep on his feet. Worden's family have gone away; his wife said she was afraid to stay there alone—

which is another fact that makes me think Worden wasn't kidnaped. She'd stay to wait for word from the kidnapers if he was snatched. So I had a flatfoot watching the place, figuring Worden might come back. This morning a car parks in front of the house. A guy in dark clothes walks up and tries the front door. He's fooling with some keys when my man yells at him. The visitor lams back to his auto and makes a getaway. The flatfoot was afraid to fire because he thought it might have been Worden trying to get into his own house. I roasted him proper, but he might have been right. Could have been Worden trying to sneak in."

Vickers agreed with Leyhan that Worden was looming bigger as a suspect. He said, "Get hold of his wife's present address. We'll have her phone tapped and her mail watched to see if she gets any word from him." Then he asked if Leyhan had heard any more from Steele.

"Not another squawk." Leyhan frowned. "Guess he's trying to find someone to haul us over the coals, the damned crack-pot!"

"I'm not so sure he is a crack-pot," Vickers said. "Steele is a shrewd bird. And he spends a lot of money for a feller that doesn't put much time in his office. We've been checking him. He's not at his place of business two hours a day. Some days he's not there at all. I'd like to know what he does with his spare time."

VICKERS received a call from Evelyn about four that afternoon. The red-headed undercover operative sounded excited as she told him that Kirk Mabie and Sara Nova had held a vehement conference in a secluded corner of the hotel lobby for about thirty minutes. Then the blonde had gone up in the elevator, but Mabie was still waiting in the lobby. It looked as if they were going out together.

"I'll grab a cab and come right over,"

Vickers said. "If they go before I get there, follow them and report in by phone."

Ten minutes later Vickers arrived at the hotel just as Mabie and the blonde entertainer came out. Mabie looked sullen and worried as he stalked across the sidewalk to a tan Chrysler parked at the curb. He slid behind the wheel, while Sara Nova stepped in and slammed the door. Evelyn followed them out and ducked into Vickers' cab, which was parked nearby.

The trail led to the North Shore Drive. Vickers whistled under his breath as the tan Chrysler turned off suddenly on to the cemetery road. He was certain from the expression he had seen on Mabie's face that this was no lovers' tryst. His hunch that the deserted graveyard fitted into the mystery was proving itself.

G-77 dismissed the cab at the junction of the cemetery road. He and Evelyn went up the road at a run, reached the top of the hill without seeing the tan sedan. Vickers swore under his breath. Had Mabie and the blonde entertainer given them the slip?

There were a dozen branching paths that the sedan could have taken. As Vickers stood, undecided as to what to do, they heard the roar of a motor. It came from near the edge of the cemetery.

They raced toward the sound, trying to make as little noise as possible as they picked their way through the brush. However, there was no car in sight when they reached the bordering road. Evelyn's exclamation of disappointment was suddenly choked by Vickers' grip on her arm. He whispered sharply, "There's a shack over there. You stay here while I investigate."

They were in the shadows of a small grove of poplars. Vickers moved out and started along the grass toward the tool shed. He had covered half the distance when the door of the shack burst open and three men stepped out and confronted him.

G-77 stopped abruptly as he glimpsed the stocky, dark-clothed man flanked on either side by hard-looking thugs. It was The Ghost! He had walked into another of the master crook's traps!

The G-man's hand whipped to his shoulder holster. He blazed a shot at the Death Dealer, dodging and whirling as he fired. If he must die he would try to take The Ghost with him. He cursed as he saw the mystery man dive back into the shack.

The gangsters drew guns with lightning speed as Vickers fired. A second later shots filled the air. But Vickers was a moving target now, racing madly in a zigzag line for the clump of poplar trees. He heard the sharp crack of a gun ahead of him, and saw Evelyn firing from the edge of the grove.

"Get back, Evelyn," Vickers screamed. "We've got to run for it."

A bullet grazed his arm as he dove into the shadows. He whirled and blazed two more shots at the pursuing thugs. One man staggered and went down to his knees. Then The Ghost plunged out of the shack with two more men at his heels. He screamed a warning and the hoods followed as he ducked for shelter behind graves and tombstones.

Dusk was closing in fast. His gun empty, Vickers whirled and raced after Evelyn who was running toward a big crypt a hundred yards distant. Vickers took a quick backward glance as he ran. He saw the white-masked man running for the shack. But the four thugs were still in pursuit.

Vickers headed for the tomb he and Tommy had investigated. He had an idea he could elude their pursuers there, and it was getting darker each minute.

He shoved Evelyn into the mausoleum, shut the door and dropped the bar in place. Then he ran to the back of the tomb and proceeded to crawl through the hole he and Tommy had discovered on their previous visit. He could hear their enemies blundering through the weeds and shrubs as he slid through the tunnel into the crypt.

"The door is barred and those bushes screen the hole in the wall. I think we can lose them here," he whispered to Evelyn.

"There are still five bullets in my gun, Lynn," she said steadily, and handed him her .25 caliber automatic.

"Only two men can come through the door at a time. I hope they try it."

VICKERS' heart thrilled at the calmness of her voice. He grinned. "You blood-thirsty little devil," he said as he took the gun from her hand.

Profane shouts outside drew near. Vickers had a bad minute when one of the thugs fumbled at the bar on the door. Another voice sneered, "Hell, they couldn't lock the door behind them, could they?" Finally the voices moved away and were lost in the distance. Vickers and Evelyn waited ten minutes, then crawled out.

"Do we go home now, or do you want to play tag some more with The Ghost?" she asked pertly.

"We'll take a look, if you feel up to doing another marathon," he said.

"Don't be silly," Evelyn said tartly. "It was my idea in the first place."

They started back toward the shack at the edge of the cemetery. G-77 halted suddenly at the sound of muffled shots. They stared at each other in amazement. The noise they heard was unmistakably the echo of gunshots. But the sound seemed to come from the ground beneath their feet!

Evelyn was the first to speak. She clutched Lynn's arm, whispered shakily, "Tell me I'm nuts, Lynn. I can feel the earth tremble. Do you suppose the stiffs are having target practice?"

Vickers wracked his brain for an explanation of the phenomenon. They made their way cautiously toward the sound. The muffled firing had ceased now.

A second later, G-77 dragged Evelyn

hurriedly into the shadow of a tombstone. Ahead of them, the door of an old vault was opening. Four shadowy figures emerged. The figure in the lead carried a leather gun-case. A pale crescent of moon slid from behind a cloud. Vickers' fingers tensed on the gun in his hand as he recognized the man with the gun case. It was The Ghost!

Rage and frustration swept through the G-man's brain. He could drop the master criminal in his tracks, but the shot would reveal their whereabouts and he and Evelyn were defenceless except for the tiny automatic. It would mean certain death for himself and the girl. The thought of letting the master crook live was like bitter gall to the G-man's mouth. But he had no right to sacrifice Evelyn March's life to realize his desire.

From the shadow of the tombstone they saw The Ghost and his men walk to the tool shed. A minute later two cars that must have been parked behind the shed started down the main cemetery road.

Vickers and Evelyn ran to the top of the hill. The cars split at the junction of the cemetery road and the Drive. One headed back to the city. The other turned down a side street off the Drive. Vickers whistled sharply. Kirk Mabie lived on that side street! Was The Ghost in the car that had gone in that direction?

His wrist watch showed 8:15 P.M. "I know you're starved and exhausted, Red Head," he said. "But there's one more job I'd like to tackle before we go."

"Well, what are we waiting for?" Evelyn snapped. "I want to see what's in that tomb as much as you do."

A big, rusty padlock clamped the iron bar in place on the door of the tomb which The Ghost and his men had just quit. But the lock had been neatly sawed through and was just there as camouflage. Vickers swung the door open, probed at the darkness with a flashlight beam. The dark interior looked innocent enough.

He turned the beam on the floor. A number of bricks had been removed, leaving uncovered boards beneath. Evelyn held the flashlight while Lynn removed them, revealing a long, slanting tunnel, just big enough for a person to crawl through.

Evelyn said shakily, "Looks like we've uncovered the secret of the graveyard, Lynn. Go ahead, I'll follow you. These clothes are ruined anyhow."

THEY slid and scrambled down a ten-foot incline. The tunnel leveled off for another fifteen feet and suddenly opened into a big cave.

Amazement widened Vickers' eyes as he helped Evelyn to her feet. They were in a natural cavern, eight feet high and nearly twelve feet wide. Erosion and the hard-packed clay over the rock bottom marked it for the dry bed of an underground river.

Flashing the beam down the cave, Vickers got another jolt of surprise. Dirt and stone from the tunnel they had just traversed had been piled in a four-foot embankment across the cave. Dark rectangles had been mounted on the embankment. Drawing closer, Vickers saw that they were plates of chilled steel. Each of the three armor plates was pierced with bullet holes. The cavern was an underground target range!

For a long minute Vickers' brain whirled dizzily. Why had The Ghost selected this weird setting for rifle practice? Then his voice thrilled with elation as he cried:

"By Heavens! I believe I've got it, Red Head! This accounts for the tomb Tommy and I investigated, also. Chesley knew this underground river bed was here. His surveying must have been faulty, for he started to tunnel through from that other tomb. Then he changed to this tomb when he realized his error."

"It's all Greek to me," Evelyn said dryly. "But I'm just a dumb dame."

Vickers outlined his theory. When he finished the girl shared his elation.

"I think you've hit it, Lynn!" she exclaimed. "But we're still in the dark as to the identity of The Ghost."

"I'll know that in twenty-four hours," Vickers promised flatly. "See if you can find any shells on the ground, Evelyn. They may have missed one or two."

A minute later Evelyn found an empty shell. Vickers found two more. Careful to avoid fingerprints, he wrapped them in his handkerchief and dropped them in his pocket.

"Those shells may furnish the evidence that will send The Ghost to the chair," he said as they made their way back through the tunnel. Falling rock and débris had sealed the cave at one end. In back of the target butt it narrowed to a tiny fissure. The subterranean rifle range was practically a sealed chamber with the tunnel as its only exit.

Despite their weary, disheveled condition, they were thrilled with the success of their venture. For Lynn Vickers believed he was near the solution of the most baffling case he had ever tackled.

CHAPTER V
The Ghost Laughs Last

TOMMY DEWART was discouraged and disheartened when he returned from Evanston. Briefly he told G-77 what he had learned about the bank raid. Two thugs had entered the bank, one watched the door while the other made the paying teller empty the drawers in the cashiers' cages. Dissatisfied with the amount of the haul, the thug had sent the cashier to the vault for more money. The panic-stricken teller reached for the police alarm and was shot down in cold blood. Then the bandit grabbed up the brief-case and raced for the door. The second thug had gunned down the watchman as he was grabbing for his gun.

Only one bit of evidence had been turned up at the bank. The killer had

been seen dropping his hand on the glass plate by the paying teller's wicket. Fingerprint men had picked up several sets of prints from this glass.

Classifications of all the prints were wired to F. B. I. headquarters at Washington. Experts there would group them, select all the cards in the file of more than five million records they had that came under the specified classifications. These cards would be run through the almost human machines for sorting. If the owners of any of the prints picked up at the bank had criminal records on file in Washington the machine would unerringly pick them out.

At ten o'clock next morning one set of prints had been identified as those of Limpy Meslin. Vickers smothered a curse. In the excitement of the robbery no one had noted Meslin's slight limp.

"That seems to eliminate Limpy as a suspect for the rôle of The Ghost," Vickers said. "He couldn't have been inside the bank and out in the car at the same time."

"Looks like Worden is elected," Tommy clipped. "But how in hell are we ever going to find him?"

"Leyhan's got a man watching his house. We may pick him up that way. But I've got another idea. Evelyn's back on the job tailing Sara Nova. I didn't have her picked up for I think she may lead us to either Limpy Meslin or The Ghost. In the meantime, I'm doing some checking myself. Guy Steele and Kirk Mabie both gave their shadows the slip last night. I want you to try and pick them up and find out where they were when Evelyn and I were in the cemetery last night. I've got a new lead that I want to follow up fast."

When Tommy had gone, Vickers put through a call to Washington. For fifteen minutes he talked to the chief of the F. B. I. He asked that an immediate search be made in the patent files and the War Department files, for possible communications from Warren Chesley regarding inventions.

It was nearly five when Vickers got a return call from Washington. His lean, tanned face registered satisfaction as he listened to the report on the bullets he had salvaged from the subterranean target gallery. At last he had the clue he needed!

He was waiting for a report from Tommy, when Evelyn called in and reported that Sara Nova was dining with Steele at a downtown hotel.

Vickers told her to stay on the job and raced downtown in a taxi to join her. At a drugstore counter across the street they ate a sandwich as they waited for Steele and the blonde to reappear.

It was nearly seven when they came out. They talked for a minute at the curb, then separated. Vickers told Evelyn to follow the blonde girl. He waited until Steele had boarded a cab, then followed in another taxi.

THE chase led across town to an Italian spaghetti house on the South Side. Vickers saw Steele wave a greeting to the man at the cashier's desk, then disappear from sight up a flight of stairs at the back of the restaurant.

Vickers passed the glass-fronted restaurant and walked to the alley beside it. Steele had just dined. Therefore the second floor of the spaghetti house must be a meeting place!

He slipped into the alley and ran to the back of the restaurant. A car without lights was parked in the narrow lane. Vickers circled garbage cans and boxes, made his way to the back door. He inched it open. Waiters were rushing from the kitchen along a narrow, dark passageway. A flight of stairs led up at his left, just inside the door. He waited until the hall was deserted, then slipped in and started up the stairs.

Light showed in only one of the private rooms on the second floor. Vickers' feet were noiseless on the shabby carpet as he moved down the hall. He bent to the keyhole and heard a gruff voice ask, "How much longer, Boss?"

Blood pounded at Vickers' temples

as he recognized the rasping tones of The Ghost as he replied: "Tonight will finish it. Then we're set for that Aurora job. If it works, nothing will ever stop us."

Vickers thought fast. There was no time to get reinforcements. There were at least four men in there, but he had to face them. He might die, but not before he had driven a bullet through the heart of the Death Dealer.

A silent prayer left Vickers' lips as he reached for the knob. He clutched the automatic in his pocket, shoved open the door, stepped inside and kicked it shut. His automatic moved in a short arc, covering the four men seated around the table.

Limpy Meslin was there, dark, ferocious and murderous. The machinegunner who had nearly blasted him down at Limpy's room was present. Vickers' gun came to halt on the fourth man, a dark figure with eyes that blazed like live coals through a ghastly white rubber mask.

"Get your hands up!" Vickers grated. "One false move and somebody heads for hell. Get 'em up!" Four pairs of hands moved jerkily upward. Blood pounded at Lynn Vickers' temples. He was going to get away with it! The Ghost was his prisoner!

Then a hoarse chuckle came from the white slit that was the masked man's mouth. "You sap!" he snapped. "Do you think I'd let a lousy punk like you trap me? You're covered by guns in the hands of my men behind ventilators on each side of this room!"

For a second Vickers was motionless. Then his eyes flashed to the side walls. He saw parts of faces framed in the dark apertures there; gun muzzles showed in the openings.

The Death Dealer's mocking voice went on: "In case you have any foolish idea about blasting me out first, forget it. Your gun is lined on the steel vest I'm wearing. Before you can lift the muzzle you'll die. Drop that gun, Vickers!"

Truth rang in the masked fiend's voice. Lynn Vickers was sick with despair and disappointment as he let his gun slide to the floor. The Ghost was indeed a genius. His defense was as perfect as his attack. No human power could ever trap this super-criminal.

"Will I rub him out, Boss?" Limpy Meslin asked eagerly.

"We don't want the cops on our neck. Put him to sleep and we'll take him out to the plant. The lye bath we had for the other dope will be the last resting place of the famous Lynn Vickers."

G-77 tried to roll away from the gun Meslin clubbed down at his head. But the gleaming barrel smashed down too swiftly. He felt a terrific explosion of pain, then everything went black.

CHAPTER VI
Death Swoops Low

WHEN Vickers regained consciousness he was on the floor of a car riding over a poorly paved street. He could see the white masked crook in front with the driver. Meslin and the other torpedo were in back. Through the fog of pain and nausea Vickers realized he was headed for a horrible finish. A bullet through his brain, then he'd be dumped into a vat of lye which would decompose both flesh and bone, leaving nothing to betray his fate.

Gradually his head cleared. He moved slightly, found that his hands and feet were bound.

Weakness and a sense of futility gave way to sullen fury. He couldn't die! If he did the Death Dealer's mob would go on, murdering, robbing and launching a crime wave that might never be checked.

The car lurched and jolted. He let his body go limp, bounce with each jolt. At the same time he strained furiously against his bonds.

The car started twisting through short blocks. He heard The Ghost say,

"Here we are. The boys are still working."

The car slued to a stop. The master crook growled, "Okay, Limpy. Take him out back and give him the works. Need any help?"

"He's still out, and he's pretty heavy. But if Frankie drives back there, I can handle him all right."

The Ghost climbed out of the car. Then Meslin's companion in the rear seat got out, kicking Vickers in the head as he did so. The G-man gritted his teeth to choke back the moan of pain. Then the car went around the corner of a low, long building, across an open space and stopped. The driver asked, "Want a hand, Limpy?"

"Help me drag him out and prop him against the wall. I can do the rest."

The two men pulled Vickers out of the car, dragged him over to a small building that looked like a warehouse. They threw him down with his back against the wall. The chauffeur got back in the car and drove away.

Limpy, meanwhile, was trying to unlock the door of the warehouse, cursing as it resisted his efforts.

G-77 waited tensely for the gangster's next move. Meslin got the door open, then reached over and gripped the collar of the G-man's coat.

Vickers came up like a man shot from a cannon. His feet were braced as Meslin started lifting. His head crashed into Meslin's stomach. Then he put everything he had into a wallop to the killer's jaw with both his bound hands. Meslin was doubling over from the blow in the stomach, when Vickers' fists clipped his chin. The gangster started back in a loop.

Pain darted up Vickers' arm as his knuckles crashed home. He fell on top of Limpy, still raining short arm jabs at the man's head. Meslin lay limp and still beneath him.

But exultation turned suddenly to apprehension as G-77 listened to the footsteps racing toward him from the shadow of the iron fence near the street.

Frantically he fumbled for the gun Meslin had dropped. His fingers were about to close around the butt when a gleeful voice called softly, "Swell work, Cotton-Top! Couldn't have done it better myself."

Lynn Vickers felt suddenly limp and washed out. "Tommy! You freckle-faced ape!" he cried weakly. "How did you get here?"

"Evelyn was worried about your trailing Steele alone. She followed you to that spaghetti joint, saw you go in, and called me. I got there in time to see them shove you in the car and drive off. The only thing I could do was trail you and hope for a break."

TOMMY slashed the bonds at Vickers' ankles as he talked. He asked, "Where do we go from here?" Will we move in on them?" He nodded to the building into which The Ghost had disappeared.

"I'd like to, Tommy, but it's too important a move to take a chance on a slip-up. We'll tie Limpy and toss him into this shack; he'll be our most important witness. Then you drive like hell to the nearest phone. Have Dan Hillary send a squad of agents armed with tommy-guns, Colt-Monitors and tear gas. Telephone Lieutenant Leyhan. He'll want to be in at the finish of the rats that murdered Jaffee. Tell them to hurry but not to use sirens. I'll stick here to tail the gang in case they leave."

It was exactly eighteen minutes later when Hillary and six agents met Vickers and Tommy outside the wire fence that surrounded the long, single-storied machine shop. It had been the longest eighteen minutes G-77 ever lived, minutes filled with fear and anxiety that the gang would move out before the raiding party arrived.

Simultaneously, Lieutenant Leyhan arrived with a squad of city detectives.

G-77 had investigated the set-up. No guard had been posted. The building had two entrances, one in front where

The Ghost had entered, and one in back near the south end of the building. The windows were screened with steel grill-work, screwed in place; there could be no escape there.

The forces were split, Hillary and Leyhan leading an attack on the rear door, while Tommy and Vickers crashed in at the front. If the doors were locked they could be shattered with automatics.

For once, Tommy Dewart's freckled face was sober, as they watched Leyhan's detachment slip silently through the shadows to the rear of the building. Vickers' men crouched by the fence, just outside the long rectangle of light cast by the ground glass windows.

Lynn Vickers' lean, set face looked keen and hard. When the two minute interval decided upon had passed, he nodded to the alert, eager men. His voice was brittle as he said, "Okay, gang. Let's go."

G-77 led the charge, Tommy at his heels. Vickers twisted the knob, hit the door with his shoulder and crashed in. Almost at the same second a shot shattered the lock of the rear door and Leyhan and Hillary crashed through.

The G-men were dazzled for a few seconds by the glare of the powerful lights over lathes, boring machines and other bulky pieces of machinery that filled the room. A hoarse voice screamed, "It's the law!" and figures ducked out of sight behind the machines. Guns flashed into action and drowned the shouts and curses of men.

G-77 yelled for his men to scatter. A bullet clipped the lapel of his coat, another burned a furrow along his ribs. A sub-machine-gun in the hands of a Federal agent broke into a death chatter. Bullets sprayed about the massive machines. Screams of wounded men mingled with the whine of bullets ricocheting off steel.

G-77's eyes went the length of the shop seeking The Ghost. In a small glassed-in office at the north end of the building he saw a pallid face pressing against a rifle stock. It was The Ghost—and this time he would not escape! Vickers dodged for a steel upright as the rifle muzzle lined on his body. As he did so he felt his left arm go limp. There was no pain, just a warm, burning sensation. He went down, rolling as he fell. Two more bullets crashed into the floor beside him. They didn't ricochet, but ploughed deep into the steel plates. It was The Ghost's gun.

Tommy Dewart cursed as Vickers fell. The lanky Bostonian grabbed a tommy-gun from a wounded agent, dropped to one knee, and blasted a hail of bullets through the office. The Death Dealer ducked from sight. Tommy ran to Vickers' side. "Lynn, are you all right?" he yelled above the roar.

"Just drilled through the shoulder, Tommy," Vickers answered, hitching himself to his knees. "How are the others doing?"

Leyhan and Hillary were advancing up the floor with their detachment, shooting as they came. The big Irishman seemed to bear a charmed life, as he dodged from post to machine and back, an automatic thundering in his fist. The crooks were giving way before the relentless fire of the law officers. A grin split Vickers' haggard face as he saw a white shirt wave suddenly above one of the machines. The Death Dealer's gang was surrendering!

As the gunfire behind them died down, Lynn motioned to Tommy to follow and started toward the glassed-in office. A burst through the wood just below the glass sent them ducking behind a machine. The big room was quiet now as tense men—both gangsters and men of the law—crouched, waiting for the duel between G-77 and the master crook to end.

"Come on out—and bring Worden with you," Vickers called to the masked man.

No sound came from the office for a minute. Then the hoarse voice of the Death Dealer called, "Don't shoot. We're coming out."

"Watch that murdering devil, Vickers!" Leyhan yelled. "He's up to some trickery. He's surrendering too easy."

But all the fight seemed gone from the masked leader. His shoulders sagged as he slunk out with his hands in the air. Behind him came the spare, gaunt figure of Seth Worden, disheveled, unkempt and hollow eyed.

PAIN was gnawing at Lynn Vickers' shoulder now. He could feel blood seeping down his sleeve. He said, "Put the bracelets on him, Leyhan, and rip off that damned mask."

Leyhan jerked the Death Dealer's hands forward and clamped on the handcuffs. His thick fingers hooked in the bottom of the white rubber mask, ripped it off. He stared incredulously. Then he said explosively:

"So Steele is The Ghost! And Worden was just working for him? I had it figured the other way round."

Vickers looked up wearily. Tommy Dewart had cut away the sleeve of his coat and shirt and was packing bandages over the wound in G-77's shoulder.

"Worden wasn't in the racket at all, Leyhan," Vickers clipped. "He was kidnaped to help Steele complete the plans of Chesley's invention."

"What in hell was the invention?" Leyhan growled blankly. "What's all this mob doing here in a machine shop?"

"Get that rifle Steele has in the office. That will give you the answer."

Leyhan went into the office and came out with the gun. At first glance it looked like a regulation Springfield .30-30. But there was an oil cup near the end of the elongated barrel, a different mechanism operated the breech and a long, flat magazine hooked just in front of the trigger guard.

"What the hell kind of a gun is this?" Leyhan said. "I know most makes, but I never saw one like this before."

"Chesley invented that gun," Vickers

said slowly. "It will drive a bullet through a piece of armor plate. The old man wanted to give it to the government. But instead, it fell into the hands of crooks when Steele, posing as a Government agent, got the plans from the old man. Then Steele rounded up a bunch of crooked mechanics and started them turning out the guns in this shop, for the mob he organized. Armed with guns like these, they blasted their way through steel doors, and ripped open bank vaults. They were almost invincible—but not quite. The original plans didn't include the repeating mechanism. The guns Steele made were single shot affairs. That's why he went back after Chesley, to get the plans for the repeating mechanism, that would make this gun the most deadly weapon that ever got into human hands. Poor old Chesley discovered then that he was dealing with crooks. You know the rest."

Seth Worden ran to Leyhan's side. "Vickers is right, Lieutenant," he said eagerly. "This fiend killed my friend Chesley, but he didn't get what he wanted. Then he kidnaped and tortured me until I was forced to devise a repeating mechanism for them."

"How about that bank robbery at Evanston? Weren't you in on that, Worden? It must have been you—all the others were accounted for."

"It was Worden," Vickers interrupted. "He was the man in the back of the car wearing the white mask. The man sitting with him had a gun on him all the time. Steele wanted to give himself an alibi, so he made Worden wear the mask at that robbery, while Steele showed himself in a Chicago night club, where a hundred or more people could give him an alibi. Just another one of Steele's clever little tricks."

"Where does Kirk Mabie fit in?" Tommy asked.

"Mabie must have told Steele about old Chesley's boast that he was going to help the government wipe out all the rats in gangland. That was when Steele started getting friendly with the old man. Then when Chesley was murdered, and I asked Mabie if he knew Steele, Mabie suspected that Steele was The Ghost. He didn't dare to say so, however, for he was afraid of being murdered too. Also, he had been the one who tipped Steele off to the invincible gun.

"So Mabie kept his mouth shut. He knew about the hidden target range; Steele had Sara Nova bring Mabie out to the cemetery to show him where it was. He wanted him there for the tryout of the repeating mechanism Seth Worden had perfected.

"That was the first actual proof I had that Steele was The Ghost. He left his fingerprints on the shells that Evelyn and I picked up there. But my proof wouldn't stand up in court. He could have said that Chesley invited him out there to try out the gun.

"I found out from Washington that Chesley had written the War Department about his invention, but it was regarded as a crank letter. No one had gotten around to checking up on it.

"Steele was so damned clever I had to trap him here and catch him redhanded. We've got our case closed now. Mabie will talk when he knows that Steele is safe behind the bars. Limpy Meslin, who was Steele's right-hand man, will do plenty of squawking before he goes to the chair. And Sara Nova, who was the contact between Steele and Limpy in arranging the robberies, will be another strong witness for the state. It cost a lot of lives—but we'll send this rat to the chair."

STEELE'S flabby face was gray. Fear had brought a craven streak to the surface.

Leyhan turned on him in disgust. "Got anything to say, rat?" he grated savagely.

The abject terror in Steele's eyes became a crafty look. Lynn Vickers stiffened as he watched the change in the white-faced murderer.

A shrill burst of insane laughter ripped f r o m Steele's throat. He screamed hoarsely:

"Yes, I've got something to say. I murdered Chesley. I tried to murder Vickers, but he was too damned lucky. He trapped me here, but he's not going to send me to the chair—"

The shrill voice slurred into unintelligible mouthings as Steele whirled and raced toward the north end of the building. Leyhan swore and plunged in swift pursuit.

Vickers watched as Steele ran toward an apparently blank wall. Then G-77 saw the manacled hands lifting, grabbing frantically at a rope hanging from one of the girders.

"Leyhan! Stop! For God's sake— hit the floor!" Vickers yelled at the top of his lungs. As he yelled, his gun whipped up and fired. The bullet struck Steele between the shoulder blades just as the insane killer's fingers closed on the rope. Vickers ducked to the floor, shouting for his men to do the same.

Leyhan was going down when an explosion rocked that end of the building. Timbers creaked, bricks catapulted about them. Dust and smoke blinded their eyes.

There was a long moment of stunned silence as all eyes turned to the gaping hole in the end wall. The steel floor plates were warped and bent. Leyhan lay quiet and still, his head and shoulders buried in the débris.

Vickers climbed to his feet, ran to Leyhan's side. Men clawed and tore at the pile of bricks and lumber. Then Tommy Dewart shouted, "Trust an Irishman for luck. Look at that!"

A steel plate had curled up just in front of Leyhan, a couple of broken joists had fallen across the plate. Most of the rocks had bounced harmlessly off these joists. The concussion had only knocked Leyhan out.

Vickers' eyes turned away from the sight at the end of the room. Fragments of Guy Steele's body were scattered through the pile of débris. The Death Dealer had made good his boast; they would never send him to the chair.

He had sprung his final trap—a can loaded with explosive, fixed on a platform on the beam above, that could be jerked down with a tug of the rope.

Vickers shivered as he looked at the remains of the mangled form of the latest Public Enemy No. 1. But for the grace of a wounded shoulder which Tommy had been bandaging, he might have been the one to pursue Steele into that trap. With no one to grasp the meaning of the wild groping of Steele's hands for the rope, the body of Lynn Vickers would have been scattered over the heap of brick and dirt. It would have been the final triumph of the man rightly named "The Death Dealer."

MERCHANTS

A COMPLETE SHORT NOVEL FEATURING THE ACES OF THE CUSTOMS NARCOTICS INVESTIGATIVE UNIT

OF PANIC

By DONALD G. COOLEY

Powerful Forces Sought To Oust G-Man Drover Dunn From His Job As He Drew Nearer To The Solution Of The Mystery Of The Black Dragons Who Were Spreading Terror And Death In San Francisco

CHAPTER I

Wings of the Dragon

THE knife hissed past Drover Dunn's ear. Its gleaming tip thudded viciously into a door a yard from his head. The haft quivered in a disappointed dance of death.

Drover Dunn crouched, hurled himself forward, twisted his lithe body in mid-air with the agility of a cat. He came around facing back along the street he had been gliding through like a spectral shadow. In his hand was an automatic, swept out from a shoulder sheath beneath Dunn's torn and dirty coat.

For a minute he stood, listening. Beneath a week-old stubble of beard his face was alert, watchful, and his icy-gray eyes stabbed savagely into the swirling gloom. Then he laughed, soundlessly and without mirth.

Somewhere ahead of him along Kearney street lay the great sprawling hulk of Chinatown. Smothering fog closed him off in a phantom world of his own. It moved in sluggish eddies, alive with vague whispers of peril, a sentient, malignant thing which drew a mocking curtain around the skulker who had hurled the deadly blade. A muffled murmur of nocturnal sounds filtered to his ears. San Francisco, at midnight, groped its way through the dripping murk like a blind and monstrous reptile.

Dunn shrugged, sheathed his pistol. His lips twisted in a sardonic smile as he stared down at his patched and shabby trousers, his cracked and ancient shoes. Few men outside of Washington had ever set eyes on Drover Dunn, ace undercover man of that select group of Federal agents known as the Customs Narcotics Investigative Unit. Even within the service he was a phantom, almost legendary figure. Tonight, when discovery of his identity would imperil the most dangerous assignment of his career, he had cloaked himself in the shabby garments and furtive shuffle of a hophead derelict.

Yet *someone had known him!* Something had gone wrong—desperately wrong!

He slipped into the shop doorway which formed an alcove from the street. The knife projected from the door frame level with his eyes. Dunn jerked it out and studied it narrowly as it lay in his palm.

It was a vicious weapon with a four-inch blade and a smooth ivory handle. A curious symbol had been printed on the ivory with a few deft brush strokes. It had the appearance of a lizard; malevolent, sinister, its gross body supported on four sharp-taloned legs.

"The Black Dragons!" Dunn whispered. His bleak eyes bored into the fog. "They've found me less than half an hour after I got off the Oakland ferry!"

A slow and merciless rage was boiling up within him at the challenge of the knife. He knew now that the blade had not been intended to cut him down —yet. It was a warning that Drover Dunn had been marked for death by the Black Dragon syndicate, that sinister brotherhood of dope and terror whose tentacles reached out to grip the Pacific Coast in a creeping paralysis of panic.

DROVER DUNN wrapped the knife in a handkerchief, dropped it in his pocket, and with huddled shoulders and hitching gait shuffled furtively down the street. The fog was his friend now as well as his enemy. It concealed him from anyone who might be following as he cut through back streets and alleys, emerging finally before a ghostly building in front of which a sickly light revealed a long flight of stairs leading interminably upward.

Dunn held his coat collar together with twitching fingers as he studied the sign "Rooms—50 Cents and Up." Under his battered hat brim his eyes pierced through the fog. He turned abruptly, shuffled up the stairs in a queer, hitching gait. A bald-headed clerk behind a desk regarded him without interest.

"A friend said he paid for a room for me," Dunn whined. "He wasn't—kiddin'? I can have it? My name's Jones."

The clerk flipped a key from the rack behind his desk.

"Number sixteen. Down the hall to your right." The clerk scowled at his shabby customer with distaste. "Six bits in advance, if you want it tomorrow night, too."

Dunn made an unintelligible croaking sound, turned down the hall and found number sixteen at the extreme end of a right angle turn. A low-wattage bulb in the ceiling made a feeble assault on creeping shadows. He turned the key in the lock, opened the door and slipped through. Bolstad, the district customs inspector, had reserved the room. If he had carried out Dunn's orders the place would have two exits.

IN the blackness some instinct urged Dunn's hand to his gun as he found the light switch and snapped it on. The automatic swept out and down in a lightning arc.

A man was sitting stiffly in a chair, facing Drover Dunn. He was a Chinese; his buttony black eyes blinking in the sudden light. He smiled faintly, his small, dapper figure quite motionless, hands lying impassively in his lap. Color deepened his sallow cheeks as he stared into the gun muzzle.

"You dirty rat, what the hell are you doing in my room?" Dunn flared. He mouthed a string of oaths—a mask behind which his brain was incisively cutting through to the purpose of the intrusion. A glance showed him another door leading out of the room, closed and bolted, a bed, two chairs, a dresser with a dirty wash basin and a window backed by the brick wall of an adjoining building.

"Me fliend," said the Chinese. "Have no gun. Maybeso you like see?"

"You're damn right I like see," Dunn snarled. Without turning, he shot home the bolt of the door behind him. "Stand up—and don't make a move."

The man got up, palms lifted outward. Dunn frisked him expertly. He carried no weapon. As Dunn's fingers strayed over the man's back, the Chinese winced and his body trembled uncontrollably. Whirling him around, Dunn was startled at the look of agony in his eyes. Sweat stood out on his parchment brow and the slant-eyed face was a sickly gray.

"I'll smash your yellow face in," Dunn raged. "I'll—"

The man smiled thinly. "No need try to fool me. I know you not hophead."

His voice quavered slightly. "You likee catch Black Dlagon?"

"What the hell are you talking about?" Dunn snapped.

"Me Ching Hong. You Dlover Dunn, smart government man. You come smash Black Dlagon. Ching Hong help."

The soft words struck Dunn with all the shock of a physical impact. A tingle of warning raced through his veins, sharpened by derisive self-mockery. Drover Dunn, phantom Federal agent, had been twice unmasked within an hour—once by an assassin who had hurled a knife, once by a bland Chinese.

"What makes you think my name is Dunn?" he asked softly.

"Only one government man smart enough to catch Black Dlagon," said Ching. "That man was Dlover Dunn. Never see your face. But Ching Hong learn you come this room tonight. I come too, wait. You come in. So I know you are Dunn."

"You're crazy as hell," Dunn snapped. "Talk some more—and *fast*."

Fever burned in Ching's glittering eyes. A spasm of pain crossed his face. His fingers dipped into his pocket and Dunn's hand streaked to his gun. But what the Chinese brought out was an object which Dunn, in frisking him, had thought was a can of tobacco.

Dunn's face was expressionless as he studied the canister. He had seen hundreds of such containers of death before. It was an opium tin!

"I bling you this, plove I your fliend." Ching's voice was earnest. "Black Dlagons want that can velly much. Do anything to get it. That tin will help you find them, take you to Ko Fat Lu. He leader of Black Dlagons. They velly bad *hui*."

Hui. Ching had used the native term for a drug-smuggling syndicate. Dunn pocketed the tin and said sharply:

"You're lying. The Dragons go in for morphine and extortion. Opium is small-time stuff for them."

"That is true," Ching Hong nodded.

"But they sell opium in Chinatown too. They want that can velly bad. Why, I do not know."

Dunn's eyes blazed. "You dirty rat! I've figured the play. You're planting this stuff on me so you can tip off the department and break me out of the service. You don't get away with it—"

"Wait!" screamed the Chinese as Dunn advanced upon him. "I tell you truth! Me belong *hui* that fight Black Dlagons for opium business. We hijack opium shipment they smuggle in. That is where I get the can."

"It's still fishy as hell," growled Dunn. "Come clean!"

Ching folded his hands, stiffened in the chair, an oddly impressive figure. "My blother Ching Lee belong Black Dlagons. They double-closs him, he commit suicide. You catch Black Dlagons, I help avenge blother's honor, he go number one heaven, join honorable ancestors."

Dunn's deep knowledge of Chinese life and customs was one factor which had made him the ace operator in the customs unit. That knowledge told him now that Ching might be telling the simple truth. If his brother had committed suicide to even a score with an enemy, only full and complete revenge would assure him a place in the Celestial heaven.

"Members my *hui* think I take this can but cannot prove." Ching's eyes glittered as he made a desperate effort to convince Dunn. "They punish me, but I still keep can—bling it to you for help. You believe—see!"

Abruptly the Chinese took off his coat and vest, stripped off his shirt and peeled down to his underwear.

Dunn choked down a startled gasp as he stared at the man's naked back. It was a criss-cross of broken, bleeding welts—the mark of the lash. The raw flesh sickened Dunn. The Chinese was bearing up under the excruciating torture with incredible stoicism.

It might be a clever trap—but it was an even chance Ching Hong had told the truth. Dunn considered swiftly. He had no intention of being found with an unexplained opium tin in his possession. Better men than he had been framed by crooks whose trails they followed too closely.

"If you've been lying, God help you," Dunn rapped out. "I'll take one chance on you, Ching. I'll take this tin, plant it in a hideout, and if you're here when I return it will help convince me you're on the level. If I'm followed, somebody gets a slug through the heart."

Ching smiled with relief. "I stay here, bolt doors inside. Black Dlagon maybe hunt me already. Feel safe here. You knock five times when you come back, I let you in."

Dunn strode to the second door and threw back the bolt. It opened on a rickety stairway leading into a vague blackness.

"Don't open to *anybody*," Dunn warned. Ching Hong slipped into a chair, nodded, but got up as Dunn stepped out and closed the door. The G-man could hear the bolt being snapped in place as he walked away.

In utter blackness Dunn felt his way down the narrow stairway, emerging into a rubbish-piled alley. He paused long enough to photograph the spot in his memory, then slunk through the *fog* and in ten minutes was in an all-night drugstore. He slipped into a phone booth and dialed a number.

"Hello . . . Bolstad?" he snapped as a gruff voice answered. "This is Murphy of San Mateo."

"Thank the Lord!" growled Bolstad as he recognized the code word.

Dunn cupped his hand around the mouthpiece. "Something's happened. I must see you at once. Can't wait till morning."

"Come right up to the house." Bolstad's voice fairly crackled. "I want to see *you*. Pick up a morning paper and you'll know why. The lid's blown off and all hell's popping!"

CHAPTER II
The Voice of Ko Fat Lu

DUNN stepped out of the booth with Bolstad's excited voice still ringing in his ears. Nothing short of an earthquake could shake Chief Inspector Conway Bolstad out of his even calm. A strange sense of uneasiness, irrational, disturbing, stirred in Dunn's veins.

He picked up a paper from a fresh pile on a counter, paid the clerk, and shuffled out. A block away he hailed a cruising owl taxi, gave Bolstad's address, and switched on the tonneau light to scan his paper.

Presently he snapped off the light, lowered the cab window and thrust the sheet into the swirling fog. In the darkness his eyes blazed with merciless, driving rage. Flaming words from the early edition seared through his brain.

EMBEZZLER CHARGES GIGANTIC NARCOTICS PLOT

Arrest of William Cotton, 41-year-old cashier of the Lumbermen's National Bank, late last evening revealed an amazing story which has spread panic through the ranks of bankers and business men throughout the Pacific Coast. Cotton confessed to the theft of $210,000 of the bank's funds.

Cotton revealed that he had unknowingly become addicted to the use of morphine in one of the most respected clubs of San Francisco. He asserted that his thefts were forced by the increasingly huge sums demanded by the agents who furnished the drug he craved.

Cotton's confession adds new fuel to rumors which have been circulating in financial circles for some weeks. An oriental narcotics syndicate known as the Black Dragon is said to have systematically debauched high executives in business organizations throughout the state, using the lever of drugs to force their victims to embezzle funds from their employers. With its sinister operations becoming known, the organization has recently expanded its activities to include extortion from business heads who are assured that for the payment of specified sums their employees will not be tampered with.

Credence is added to these rumors by the fact that a wave of embezzlements has recently wrecked several banks and business houses in San Francisco. It is feared that operations of the Black Dragon have drained colossal sums from institutions which will not be disclosed until an army of auditors makes a thorough check. Panic has begun to spread through the city as the vast extent of the most diabolically clever racket in the nation's history becomes known . . .

Dunn crouched on the edge of the seat, feeling suddenly alone, helpless. That newspaper story was going to make things tougher. It meant that he was going to have a pitifully short time in which to work, with the odds all against him. His mind cut like a rapier through the maze of rumors to the one word *panic!* Bank runs, failures, fears —a colossal crash that would shake the nation to its foundation.

The cab dropped him off before a house where lights glowed behind curtained windows. He was admitted by Bolstad himself.

"Dunn — t h a n k God!" Bolstad's square-jawed face was drawn and haggard. He had never seen Dunn and he studied the bearded, shabby figure through bloodshot eyes. "I'm glad you've come, damned glad!"

Dunn followed the inspector into a library, quieted the inspector's nervousness by plunging straight to business.

"I came to bring you this." Dunn handed Bolstad the opium tin. "Little memento from a Chink named Ching Hong. Found him waiting for me a few minutes ago, *in my room.*"

Bolstad got the undercurrent of the words.

"You think—there was a leak in the department?" Bolstad furrowed his fingers through his hair. "I—I can't believe it, Dunn."

"Ching Hong knew I was coming to that room," Dunn clipped out. "Figure your own answer." Briefly he went over Ching's story, and as Bolstad nodded silently he added, "I came here to turn that opium tin over to you as my superior. You can guess why?"

Bolstad walked to a taboret and poured himself a drink. "It *has* happened; men who were *too* good framed out of the service." He wheeled, his gaze piercing through the Federal agent. "That won't do for you, Dunn. You're all we can count on now—our ace-in-the-hole. You've got to keep that tin. Don't you see it's our only real clue?"

"Is it?" asked Dunn abruptly.

Bolstad stared at him strangely. "What do you mean by that?"

"You have your stoolies. You have a hundred crack agents. As chief of the district you must have some idea where this dope tin is smuggled in."

"We's knocked off small peddlers; little shots." Bolstad spread his hands helplessly. "It hasn't brought us a step closer to the brain behind it. We've heard his name—Ko Fat Lu. But we don't know what he looks like, how he operates, where his headquarters are—"

"What you're trying to say is, I'm starting cold?"

"Not exactly." Bolstad's eyes fired. "That opium tin—there's something to it. There *was* a suicide down on Pacific street two weeks ago. A Chink named Ching Lee."

Dunn restored the tin to his pocket. "It may be a clue or a death trap. I'll soon find out. But you and I know opium isn't the Dragon's racket."

Bolstad grimaced. "If it only were! No, it's morphine—extortion—panic! You read the papers. There are thirty other cases as bad as Cotton's, but we've kept them under cover. Now the Dragons know their power. They've got every business man in town in a cold sweat. I tell you, they're wrecking the city!" His fingers tightened on Dunn's arm. "You'll find out how the terror's spreading soon enough. Robert Haig just phoned he's coming over. He owns several banks, has a finger in half the town's affairs—"

"*Here?*" Dunn cried sharply. "You know I never show my face in public! Get me out of the way."

Bolstad's surprise dwindled. "Yes, yes—I had forgotten. You're a phantom, Dunn. Thank God you are." His glance rested on a large silk screen beside a fireplace. "You ought to listen in. We can move that screen to a corner. You can hear without being seen."

DUNN nodded swiftly. They moved the screen and he discovered he could see most of the room through a crevice. Bolstad paced the floor restlessly. The minutes dragged.

A peal from the doorbell clanged through the house. Dunn could hear a bull-voiced man greeting Bolstad. The pair came into the library. Dunn studied Haig curiously. The banker was a heavy, florid type, chunky in build, with sharp blue eyes which didn't miss a trick. He moved restlessly about the library with animal-like grace, gesturing with a maul-like fist.

"I've come straight to you, Bolstad, because I'm damned tired of the way you Federal men crawfish and throw out a lot of promises. Cotton is into me for a quarter of a million—the Lumbermen's National is my bank. What's worse, there have been three other cases like his in my own businesses—and God knows how many others around town! It's got to stop, I tell you. If you don't smash these Black Dragons—" Haig choked apoplectically, fixed Bolstad with a furious eye.

"Not two hours ago I got a telephone call. The devils had the guts to tell me that for two hundred thousand dollars *they wouldn't make any more money demands* from men of mine they've been hopping up with their cursed dope! The damned colossal nerve—" Haig choked in his anger. "I told him to go to hell."

"*Him?*" Bolstad asked.

"Ko Fat Lu. That's what he said his name was—*Ko Fat Lu*. A damned oily Chinese voice. He's a man, Bolstad. He's human. He's somewhere in San Francisco—and it's your job to run him down."

Why didn't Bolstad shoot out questions—where the call had come from, the exact hour, precisely what had been said? Dunn boiled inwardly, restraining himself with an effort from bursting out to take charge. The inspector looked beaten, haggard, as he stood and took it.

"Dope's at the bottom of it, Bolstad!" The table groaned under the impact of Haig's fist. "Morphine! It's smuggled in. You customs men could stop it in a minute if you wanted to. I want to know what you intend to do?"

"Perhaps we're doing more than you think," said Bolstad wearily.

Haig shot him a shrewd glance. "You mean you've got a smart agent on the job at last?"

But Bolstad was not to be cornered. "This is the toughest situation I've ever seen in thirty years in the customs service," he said. "Give us time."

"Time—time!" the banker yelled. "Do you realize, man, that in twenty-four hours every bank in the city may be forced to close its doors? The newspapers have got hold of the story now. You'll see rioting by morning—and murder."

Haig sat down, drumming his fingers heavily on a table top.

"Don't look so startled. Maybe I'm crazy. This thing's driving me mad. But one of my best friends—Blanchard of the Drover's Exchange—was found dead in his bed last week. I happen to know his bank had been hit pretty heavily. Four trusted men practically walked off with the contents of the cash boxes. The autopsy report was poison, unidentifiable. Blanchard never killed himself. He was murdered by Ko Fat Lu!"

The whiteness of Bolstad's face startled Dunn. The inspector tossed off another drink, poured one for Haig. It quieted the banker. He shook his head wearily.

"I—I'm about done up. I had to warn you, Bolstad. I expect action. I'll be down at your office in the morning for a full report."

When the door closed on Haig, Dunn came out from behind the screen.

"The man's right, Bolstad," he said quietly. "It's bad business. I think I'd better get into action with my little tin can." He snapped off the lights, paused at the door. "Anything to this business about Blanchard, or was Haig just excited?"

BOLSTAD'S shaken voice drifted out of the darkness. "I don't know, Dunn. The facts are as he stated them. There was no sign of a poison container, and servants swore no one had entered the house. It—it may have nothing to do with the Black Dragon."

Dunn shrugged. "Good night," he said, and stepped out into the darkness. He cut through to the back of the house, walked a block down an alley, and found a cab. It dropped him off two blocks from the rooming house, and he covered the rest of the distance on foot. The fog was thinning.

He felt his way up the dark rear stairway. He tapped lightly on the door at its head, five times. There came no answer. Dunn repeated the signal, more sharply. Ching Hong might have fallen asleep. He counted sixty dragging seconds, tried again to no avail.

"Lammed!" Dunn gritted. "The yellow devil!"

Gun in hand, he crashed his shoulder to the door. The wood was stout. Four times he hurled his steel-sprung weight against it before the sheath of the bolt ripped loose.

The light still burned inside. The room was exactly as he had left it, except that Ching Hong was lying on the floor staring at the ceiling from glazed, horror-filled eyes. His figure lay in a convulsive huddle, one hand clutching at his shirt which he had ripped open in his agony.

Dunn went down on one knee. His hand went to Ching Hong's breast.

The man was dead.

CHAPTER III

Opium Code

DUNN was on his feet in an instant, sweeping the room with a stabbing gaze which missed nothing. The very air of the room was heavy, dead, freighted with a stagnant exhalation of peril.

The other door was still bolted, as had been the one he had crashed. The single window was locked. Dunn lifted the sash and peered out. A solid brick wall was a scant six inches away. It was impossible for a human body to have squirmed down that narrow crevice.

Again Dunn knelt beside the body. He found no sign of a wound, nor any indication of a container which might have held a draft of poison. The raw wounds on Ching's tortured back could not have brought death so swiftly. How then had he died—and why?

"The Dragons got him," Dunn murmured, and choked off the words on a sudden thought. "Or did they think they were getting *me?*"

His head throbbed painfully as he tried to think the thing through. His senses were sluggish. Ching Hong might have been his unwitting proxy in a rendezvous with death. However the man had died, Dunn had to get out of there in a hurry. The torture marks on Ching's back would give the newspapers a front page sensation. For Dunn to be questioned in any way would mean certain exposure of his identity, which would prove fatal to his present purpose.

Dunn swayed dizzily as he stumbled to the stairway door. His fingers touched his brow and came away wet with perspiration. His head was splitting, his stomach heaving.

In a half-daze he groped his way down to the back alley, wondering at his sudden illness. The cool air revived him somewhat. Curious, that sudden deadly nausea that had gripped him. He had thought himself hardened to the sight of sudden death.

He walked slowly to the Grand Palace Hotel. A beefy house detective sauntered toward him with his cigar cocked at a belligerent angle.

"I'll have a little snappy coöperation," Dunn clipped out. "Room and bath. Have a bellhop, my size, up there in ten minutes."

The dick's cigar dropped as his bulging eyes scanned the Federal badge in Dunn's palm. He favored the bearded derelict with a glance of respect, accepted a proffered ten-spot, and came back with a key after consulting the night clerk.

"Number 641," the dick said. "I'll show you up." Before the door on the sixth floor he blurted, "There ain't any trouble? That is—"

"Not if you keep the old mug buttoned," said Dunn. "I'll be looking for that bellhop."

In his room Dunn stripped off his shabby clothes, ran his hand over the stubble of beard. A knock sounded at the door. He admitted a six-foot, red-headed bellhop.

"You'll do," said Dunn, measuring him. The figure "50" showed on a bill peeping through his fingers. "Fit yourself to a new suit of clothes and bring 'em in to me. Also a razor, blades, and electric soldering iron, and every kind of solder you can lay your hands on."

"Jeez!" breathed the bellhop.

"Can you do it; or can't you?" the G-man snapped.

"Sure I can," the bellhop said excitedly. "Borrow 'em from the carpenter in the basement."

Dunn slapped him on the back, starting him toward the door. When he was gone Dunn picked up the phone and called Bolstad's number.

"Bad news, Bolstad," he announced. "Ching Hong was dead when I got back. Must be suicide. Nobody cracked into the room; it was sealed tight. Tip off the cops and be sure you have a chemical analysis made. I think he died from poison. I want to know pronto."

"Do you realize," Bolstad gasped, "they may have been after *you?*"

"I've thought of that," Dunn admitted dryly, and hung up.

In his hand he held the opium tin he had carried in his coat. It was in no apparent respect different from a

"Maybe *that's* what makes it different," he murmured. "That—or something inside!"

THE bellhop returned at that moment with a neat gray suit and a paper sack which he clanked down on a writing desk.

"Nice work," Dunn approved.

"Duck, Haig! Duck!" Dunn yelled to the b a n k e r. (Page 64)

hundred other contraband containers.

"Standard five tael capacity. Wait a minute!" He whistled sharply. His eyes made out two tiny dents in the bottom ridges of the can where the side was crimped to the base. The indentations were slight, as if a hatchet or some similar object had been tapped lightly against the exposed edges.

He locked the door after the bellhop and poured out the contents of the bag. It held a soldering iron, a razor, package of blades, strip solder and several cans of liquid compounds.

Spreading a newspaper on the desk, he stood the opium tin upright upon it. With one of the blades he cut the base of the tin in a clean, sharp line.

If there was anything in that can to interest the Black Dragons, Drover Dunn was going to know about it first!

He groaned with disappointment when, after twenty minutes, he was able to bend up the tin base and study the stuff inside. It was a gummy, viscous substance with a sickly-sweet scent. He dipped a fingertip into it and rubbed it on the newspaper.

"Number one Malwa opium," he muttered. "Smuggled in from Macao, probably. Can't be worth over a hundred bucks. Did Ching Hong give me a bum steer?"

He dabbed at the poppy-gum resentfully. Some foreign substance in it resisted his finger solidly. Dunn's eyes contracted into pinpoint pupils and his breathing came swiftly. He inserted thumb and forefinger into the viscous mass. They closed on something solid. He drew it out, stringy masses of opium dripping back into the can.

At first, covered as it was by the sticky drug, Dunn could not make out the nature of his find. It seemed to be a small rectangle about the size of a playing card. He carefully wiped off the surplus opium and found himself holding a hopelessly stained piece of cardboard. Dunn studied it narrowly. If there had been a message of any sort on its surface, the opium had rendered it forever illegible.

"They'd foresee that, whoever put this thing in the can," Dunn mused. "I wonder—"

Suddenly he took the razor blade and sliced off a tiny sliver from the edge of the cardboard. A gleam of satisfaction lighted the cold depths of his eyes. The slice showed plainly that the cardboard was comprised of two flat pieces, glued together at their edges. Dunn inserted the blade between the two plies and pried them apart.

Tiny veins throbbed at his temples. His smile was wry, ironic as he stared at the small square of rice paper which had rested between the two bits of cardboard. He had found the secret of the opium tin, only to come face to face with a greater puzzle.

The paper was covered solidly with a haphazard jumble of letters. A typewriter had been used to imprint the alphabetical symbols. They danced mockingly before Dunn's eyes as he studied them:

```
lsngtuhcwfddbhjanzuwwiomrinev
cbxcubetbvayxvuebahbploiencus
nunbohjnabxerbnlponqfgudszhya
oeesjmkqtrvuoixlurrnrbalbypfm
gfowbprcehdoobwitauibxpoberna
qivnejrakluimebatyrpolknieran
xclepniubtzrlrunihainbbohmape
imolyshitrebvshnbliedzjnllibo
bcfqjiloncmreydghkciniawdrofl
tmiultafokbtrraqhbenhtbbwxuea
asecegnohepiptrelblapmircyofb
kitihaiteeplhfeztarblenihfjwl
```

For long minutes Dunn stared unseeingly into space. The thing baffled him. It followed no recognized principles of cryptography that he was aware of. There were no breaks to indicate words, no clue as to whether it was a transposition or substitution cipher. It might be broken down by a tedious mathematical process—but time was pitifully short.

Dunn concealed the opium tin and its contents in the desk drawer and sent down a call for the red-headed bellhop.

"One more little job for you," he said when the boy appeared. "I need a typewriter in a hurry. It doesn't matter what kind, but it must be a machine with small type. Elite letters, they call it."

"Okay." If the red-head was surprised at the extraordinary nature of Dunn's errands, he gave no sign. He returned shortly with a portable machine and left Dunn to his mysterious devices.

TEDIOUSLY the Federal agent made two exact copies of the message on the rice paper. It took a long time, for he had to be sure he made no errors in transcribing it. When he had finished he compared his result with the original. They were identical even in size, the type of the two machines being almost a perfect match.

"One thing it proves, at least," Dunn reflected. "The message is probably in English. No Chinese ideographs mixed in. Which means either that Ko Fat Lu does business in English, or that he works with white men."

It proved simple enough to restore the message to its original condition and replace it in the tin, but when Dunn connected the iron and attempted to solder the tin base back in place he met with trouble. The heat caused the drug to bubble up in a hopeless gummy mass. He worked for an hour, grimly, face tightening in lines of desperation. It was imperative that he cover up every indication of his tampering.

It was four o'clock before he finally succeeded, using a can of patent liquid solder the bellboy had included in the assortment. In the end it was not a perfect job, but it would have to do.

He burned the newspaper in the washbowl, washing down every trace of opium with the ashes. Unscrewing a chandelier, he concealed the tin in its hollow base and lay down to catch a fitful catnap.

It was seven when he awakened. He shaved, got into his new suit, and studied himself in the mirror. The derelict of the night before had vanished.

He retrieved the opium tin from the chandelier, restored his gun to its shoulder sheath, and went out to a dairy lunch for breakfast. Before him, as he ate, was propped a morning paper. Panic ran through the frenzied news stories like a sinister red thread.

Flashes of headlines, fragmentary sentences seared themselves into his brain. "Panic Threatens Financial Marts—Depositor Runs Feared—Audits Reveal Four More Embezzlements—Organizations Honeycombed by Black Dragon Victims—Extortion Methods Revealed—Gigantic Conspiracy Runs Into Millions—Murder Hinted—"

Murder! A news-hawk had got hold of the story of Blanchard's death; played it up. The panic-stricken accounts seeped into Dunn's veins with the contagion of a virulent toxin. He felt alone, disarmed, threatened. Before him was the mental image of queues of frantic depositors lined up before cashiers' windows. And to combat that sinister society of looters Drover Dunn had a tin of opium, an indecipherable message, and the dubious story of Ching Hong!

He went out of the restaurant with his jaw set, found a side-street haberdashery and purchased a new shirt, hat, and pair of shoes, donning them in a dressing room. Then he headed straight for a phone booth and called Bolstad's office.

"I've got to see you at once," Dunn said guardedly. "You'll find me in the plaza in front of City Hall in thirty minutes."

DUNN walked leisurely up Market Street, found a bench in the square at the city's municipal center, and sat watching the pigeons thoughtfully. In a few minutes Bolstad arrived, eyes dark-circled from lack of sleep. He was extremely nervous and he avoided Dunn's eyes.

"Haig and a bunch of civic pillars will be swarming down within an hour on my office," he stammered unhappily. "And what can I tell them? Nothing! Dunn, this damned thing is getting me—my nerves are shot. It's unbelievable. The Black Dragon is the most powerful force on the Pacific Coast at this minute."

"Stall Haig—promise him anything," Dunn bit out. "I have an idea, Bolstad, that may work. And also a little job for you."

He handed Bolstad one of the typed copies of the opium cryptogram.

"I found that in Ching Hong's little present," he said laconically. "Teletype it to the F. B. I. in Washington. The D. J. boys there have cipher experts who can crack it if anybody can. Tell 'em it's life and death."

The inspector's eyes devoured the bit of paper hungrily.

"Dunn, it must be in English! Do you suppose Ko Fat Lu—"

"I can't afford to suppose anything," Dunn bit out. "What about the autopsy on Ching Hong?"

"That's something else that gives me the jitters." Bolstad shivered. "Not a mark on the body except those lash marks on his back. Yet—" Bolstad's voice dropped to an agonized whisper—"The chemist says he'd swear the Chink died from *snake bite!*"

The G-man looked startled. For an instant he was beyond words.

"It's fantastic — a mad nightmare!" Bolstad gasped. "The analysis showed traces of a poison. It acted swiftly on the nervous system, destroyed the blood corpuscles—exactly like cobra venom!"

"Snake bite? Sounds more like dragon bite to me." Dunn smiled sardonically, but his face was suddenly bleak, expressionless. "Have 'em check up on Blanchard. If he died the same way we've hooked his death to the Dragons; proved it murder."

Bolstad nodded feebly, staring at his shoes.

"When the banks open in an hour the panic will begin." Dunn spoke slowly, tonelessly. "There's one gamble I can take. It's clear that whatever the meaning of that cryptogram, the Black Dragons will move heaven and hell to get it. It's my habit to play a lone hand, Bolstad. It's just possible I can find the joker in the cards."

He leaned forward, his voice all but inaudible now, holding Bolstad's startled attention with a piercing gaze.

"Live bait—a death gamble—with me and the opium tin offered up as sacrifices. I want you to give me half a dozen of your crack agents. They'll spread the word in underworld circles that I have the tin. I'll make it clear where I can be found at a certain hour. That bait will draw the Dragons out of their holes. And when they close in on

me you can follow the devils to their den."

Bolstad touched his dry lips with his tongue. His eyes burned feverishly. "I —I'm afraid we can't work it, Dunn. I can't help you with my men. That's— something I had to tell you. I got this wire a few minutes before you called."

He was crumpling a yellow sheet in his twitching fingers. Dunn's rapier-like glance caught a Washington dateline.

"Ko Fat Lu—the Black Dragons— must have framed you," Bolstad stammered. "It's my orders to suspend you from the service. They've broken you!"

CHAPTER IV
Ambuscade

DUNN'S swelling rage, merciless and terrible, found expression in a flashing reflex which drew his face into a taut mask. Then he laughed softly, relaxed against the bench, watching Bolstad from half-closed eyes.

"What are you going to do about it?" Dunn asked softly.

"Maybe there's one way out," Bolstad suggested jerkily. "If you don't report to the office, I can't very well fire you."

Dunn closed his eyes. He could hear Bolstad's heavy breathing. For twenty-four hours, perhaps, he could play the game as the inspector suggested.

His eyes snapped open. "Okay, Bolstad. You get going on the decoding of that message. I'll be on my way."

"But, Dunn—what are your plans?" the inspector demanded anxiously. "I've got to know where you are, what you're doing! When the Dragons learn you're carrying that tin you'll be in frightful danger. A word from you and I'll have a dozen men on the run to help—"

"I'll keep you posted by telephone," Dunn promised. "You'd better be getting back to the office."

Bolstad seemed unwilling to have him go. His tired eyes were anxious.

"You won't fail to let me know just what you're doing?" he insisted. "I'm taking a chance too, Dunn, failing to obey orders."

Dunn grinned, slapped him on the back reassuringly, and stared after him narrowly as he walked off. The inspector seemed the least bit overanxious. It was natural for Bolstad to wish to keep in close touch with Dunn, and yet— Unbidden suspicions stirred restlessly to life.

Could Bolstad have been reached? Only a departmental leak could have given Ching Hong his tip-off on the room Dunn was to occupy, The war chest of the Black Dragons ran into millions. Men had been bought and sold for fractions of that sum. And in the order for his suspension Dunn had convincing proof that the merchants of panic had reached their tentacles into high places and convinced honest men that he was a renegade.

"You're on your own with a vengeance, brother Dunn," he murmured.

It was a quarter past eight when the G-man strolled out of the plaza, hailed a cab, and was dropped off within a block of Ching Hong's death chamber. A day clerk had replaced the bald-headed key-keeper of the night before and when Dunn had presented his credentials he turned over the key to room sixteen. The G-man went up to the same room he had left but a few hours ago in his rôle of shabby derelict.

Alone, Dunn sat down in the chair Ching Hong had occupied not many hours before. The police had done a pretty thorough job of mussing up. The bed was torn apart, dresser drawers hung open, and the threadbare rug had been rolled up and left in a heap.

Dunn lit a cigarette and smoked idly with half-closed eyes, reconstructing a mental picture. The doors bolted, windows locked, Ching Hong sitting in the chair.

"It couldn't have been a live snake,"

Dunn mused. "No fang marks. No space under the doors to crawl in. No transom."

The G-man recalled the splitting headache and feeling of nausea that had gripped him when he found the body. Almost as if there had been poison in the air . . .

His eyes shot open, bright, penetrating. From where he sat his glance fell naturally on a bit of brass tubing extending from the wall, head-high.

"By the Lord—I've got it!" He sprang from the chair as if it had been suddenly electrified.

The end of the brass tube had once been plugged with a wax-like substance. A few traces remained. It was obviously part of a gas fixture which had not been used since the building was wired for current. Several powder-like particles adhered to the inside of the muzzle-like tube. Dunn inserted a fingertip gingerly, drew it out. Several yellowish-white crystals clung to his skin. He brushed them off carefully with a grimace of distaste.

Then, closing the door, he went out for a talk with the clerk.

"There's a room directly above sixteen," Dunn clipped out. "I want the key. Who occupied it last night?"

"That would be room thirty-two." The clerk handed him a key, studied a grimy register. "The name here is Frank Black—"

THE name was meaningless. Dunn walked up a stair to the floor above, found room thirty-two a twin to sixteen just below it. The bed had not been slept in, but the floor was littered with cigarette butts. Dunn poked his head through the single window and stared down. Below was the window of room sixteen. At night the light in room sixteen would cast a rectangle of illumination on the adjoining brick wall

From where he stood it would be easy to observe the shadow of anyone moving about below.

Here, too, there was a disused gas jet in the wall. The cigarette butts were clustered beneath it. Dunn's keen eyes scanned the baseboard at the floor level. It was warped, broken and loosely fastened to the wall.

HE dropped to one knee and tugged at the board. It came away easily in his hands. Behind it was a jagged hole cutting through the lath and plaster. Dunn lay flat, reached an investigating arm through the hole and felt his way around nails and lath-ends. His fingers closed on the open end of a metal tube a couple of feet below the floor level. From its position he was certain it was the jet opening into room sixteen.

"So that's how it was done," he muttered. "The dirty devils!"

Dunn shivered. He knew now the diabolical manner in which Ching Hong had died, but that knowledge had brought him no closer to the Black Dragons.

He went down the stairs, gave the key to the clerk, and in the street outside discovered that it was past nine o'clock. Haig and his fellow bigwigs would probably still be in consultation with Bolstad. Dunn looked up the address of the Lumbermen's National Bank, found it was some ten blocks away, and set out to walk the distance.

"Looks like a longshore riot," he muttered as he caught sight of a milling mob fighting for admittance to the bank's grilled lobby. A score of patrolmen, night-sticks in hand, struggled to maintain order. Dunn's face tightened as the sullen, fear-drenched voice of the mob droned into his ears. He realized he was witnessing the first of the Black Dragon riots.

On the fringe of the crowd the G-man leaned against a building and waited. Frantic faces, lined with fear and soul-shaking panic, swirled around him. these people were small depositors who feared the closing of the bank and the loss of their life savings.

Dunn saw Haig's black limousine while it was still a block away. A white-faced chauffeur pushed the car at a crawl through a narrow space cleared by anxious police officers. As the machine fought its way to the curb, Dunn, jerking open the rear door, stepped in and sat down beside the startled banker.

"I'm a Federal agent," the G-man said quickly. "We can waste time arguing the point, or talk while we're driving out of here. What's your answer?"

Robert Haig's eyes measured him in a glance that had the bite of cold steel. He grunted, nodded, leaned back in his seat.

"Get us out of this, Bert," he called to the driver. He turned to Dunn suspiciously. "I've just come from Bolstad's office. Who are you?"

Dunn wasted no words. "Bolstad may not have been the man for you to go to. I work right out of Washington. I come to you directly because there may be good reasons for my not mixing in with Bolstad."

The shot struck home. Dunn watched the purple tide of color rush to Haig's cheeks.

"The double-crossing grafter! I *thought* he could have put a stop to this smuggling business if he hadn't been bought—"

Dunn interrupted him with curt, staccato sentences. "What I tell you is confidential. Bolstad may be okay; I don't know. But I can't take chances. I've come to you as the one man who can help me. My job is to run down the Black Dragons. And—" His voice lowered to a gentle murmur— "I understand you have heard the voice of Ko Fat Lu."

Haig's pudgy hand doubled into a fist.

"The yellow devil threatened me," he growled. "I told him—"

Dunn broke in, "Have your driver head for a highway. We can tell better if we're being followed."

The banker cast a harried glance through the rear window. "Head toward the house, Bert," he ordered, and explained to Dunn, "My estate is a few miles out near the beach. Now—how can I help you?"

"Ko Fat Lu demanded money. How and where were you to pay it?"

"I don't know. I told him to go to hell."

"That," said Dunn softly, "was before Cotton confessed?"

"Yes." Haig wiped his brow. "I had our books gone over after I got Ko Fat Lu's threat. That's how we tripped Cotton. How many more like him we have on the staff I don't know."

THE car was making its way swiftly out of the city. Dunn was silent for a minute. Then he asked, "You traced the call?"

"To a pay booth in the Ferry Building," Haig said.

"Not much of a lead there. But it at least proves that Ko Fat Lu operates in Frisco. What did his voice sound like?"

Haig frowned. "Why, sort of Chinese. Oily. Sing-songy."

"That's a big help," said Dunn dryly. He leaned forward and tapped Haig's knee. "I didn't really think you could tell me much. I want you to help me in another way."

"I'm your man," Haig growled. "Those devils are ruining me. I may be bankrupt now for all I know. I'll give my last cent to see them in hell!"

"It won't be necessary," Dunn drawled. "There's one thing the Black Dragons would sell their souls for. A tin of opium. A *particular* tin. I know where I can lay my hands on it."

Haig choked down a cry, his eyes apprehensive. "You don't mean—you're carrying it with you?"

"Think I'm a fool?" Dunn snapped—and his arm pressed against the inner coat pocket in which the tin rested. The car was turning off the highway into a macadam road, leaving the string of traffic behind.

"You're a big shot, Haig. You have friends on the police force. You can pull strings to get certain information broadcast to the underworld." Dunn smiled ironically. "At nine o'clock tonight I shall start from the Ferry Building and walk up Market Street. I'll be carrying the tin of opium. You're to spread the word so the Black Dragons will be sure to pick me up. I'm the bait in the rat trap, Haig."

He paused for a pregnant instant. "You will also have me trailed by a squad of the smartest plainclothesmen in the city. They're to tail me—see where I'm taken—and exactly one hour after I'm in the Dragons' den they're to raid the building."

Haig smacked an exultant fist into his palm. "By God, we can do it! A sweet trap! But nine o'clock—that may be too late." His heavy face clouded anxiously. "I hate to think what a day's run on the banks may do. Couldn't you make it earlier? Get your opium tin *now*—"

Dunn shook his head absently. Out of the corner of his eye he had caught a glimpse of a sleek black sedan trailing far behind them. The macadam road was no longer a straight ribbon, but a winding trail following the contour of the hills.

"You'll need a few hours to spread the word." Dunn's ominous glance alarmed Haig. *"We're being followed,"* the agent added quickly.

The banker moved his graying face to the center of the rear window, stared back. Dunn jerked him viciously to the seat.

"Keep out of sight, you fool! Have you a gun?"

"No," Haig choked. "You think—you mean they'll—"

"Keep to your side of the road," Dunn ordered the driver. "Give 'em plenty of room to pass. If they try to crowd you, crash into them."

They were crawling around a curve at a ten-mile pace. And then, swiftly, Dunn had his answer. The shadow of the black sedan purred up alongside them. He caught a flashing glimpse of its occupants—two men in each seat, all unmistakably Chinese. The man beside the driver held a gun on Haig's chauffeur.

Bert yelled, jammed on his brakes so swiftly that Dunn was thrown against the back of the front seat. He came up from his crouched position with his gun unslung. Haig was bellowing, scrambling toward the door.

The black sedan disgorged two evil-faced Chinese from the rear seat. Both of them held guns. One of them jerked open the limousine door. Dunn, his gun swinging to bear on the man, cursed silently as Haig's body rose in the line of fire. The banker had been jerked to the ground from the running board of the limousine.

The Chinese, satisfied that Bert was cowed with terror, turned to join his comrades. Dunn flipped a quick shot at him. The man groaned, slumped back in his seat. The driver beside him kept his hands on the wheel, ready for a getaway.

"Duck, Haig—*duck!*" Dunn yelled. The banker was putting up a fight with the two Chinese. A gun barrel flashed, crashed down on Haig's head. The banker groaned, slumped to the roadside.

DUNN was half-crouching in the tonneau of the limousine. His gun spat once. The slug shattered the rear window of the black sedan. The two thugs twisted around to face him. Strangely, they held their fire, but one of them trained his pistol on the moaning figure of Haig.

"You come out or we shoot your friend!" he yelled to the G-man.

Dunn saw the play. They didn't want to shoot *him*—they wanted him alive! Had they known he carried the opium

tin in his pocket they wouldn't have been quite so particular.

"Okay!" Dunn yelled. "You've got me! I'm coming out!"

His arms were lifted as he stepped to the running board, his gun pointed harmlessly at the sky. The muzzle which had menaced Haig swung to cover Dunn. The other Chinese, a husky six-footer, moved toward the G-man.

The Federal agent leaped into action with the speed of light. His gun came down on the nearest man's skull. The fellow let out a moan, but did not drop. Dunn fended him off with a straight left. The pistol slipped from the dazed Chinaman's fingers. Dunn swung his gun on the remaining thug and cursed fervently as Haig, dazed and staggering, stumbled to his feet, swaying in front of the target. Behind Haig the Chinese was taking careful aim at Dunn.

It was risky, but there was no other way out. The gun bucked in Dunn's hand. A high-pitched scream told him he had put his slug through a tiny opening that had showed for a flashing instant between Haig and the Chinese. The Chinese's gun dropped from nerveless fingers, his wrist gushed blood.

A powerful arm encircled the G-man in a bear-like grip, pinning his gun arm. The thug he had slugged was swinging into action. Dunn heaved, broke the grip, lashed out blindly. As they struggled he saw the other Chinese streaking for the safety of the sedan.

His hands closed on his assailant's throat. The man gasped. Dunn's knee came up in a savage jerk, caught him in the stomach. The Chinese sagged to his knees, groaning. Dunn knelt to the ground, seeking his gun which had dropped in the struggle. He saw it, finally, some ten feet away. He streaked toward it, picked it up.

He swung around just as the black

sedan, with a roar, raced down the road. Dunn's victim had managed to drag himself through the door. Dunn's gun spat flame and the rear window of the fleeing car, shattered. He aimed at the tires, emptying the automatic. The careening target disappeared around the bend.

Dunn sheathed his gun, helped Haig to the limousine, The banker was red-faced, boiling with fury.

"The Black Dragon picked up the trail too soon." Dunn said, helping Haig into the car. As he stepped to the running board his glance picked up an object wedged under the rear tire. He knelt quickly, picked it up. It was a brown billfold. Swiftly he pocketed it and stepped into the car.

"Back to town, James," said Dunn laconically, to the white-faced driver.

Haig was ominously silent as they raced back to the city. The beating he had taken rankled.

"We'll meet 'em again," Dunn promised grimly. "Or *I* will. Get your lines out as soon as we get back, Haig. Remember the word you're spreading—I'll leave the Ferry Building at nine sharp. And the police are to raid the den I lead them to in exactly one hour after I enter it. *One hour.* Is that clear?"

"Count on me," Haig exploded savagely. "Somebody's going to pay for cracking me on the head."

CHAPTER V
The Lattice

DROVER DUNN'S course, as he left Haig's car on upper Market Street, was a curiously tortuous one which brought him eventually to a quiet hotel on Nob Hill where he engaged a room. He did not dare return to the Grand Palace. Possibly it was there that the Black Dragon had picked up his trail. His temporary victory left him with no illusions of security.

In the seclusion of his room he examined the billfold which was his sole trophy of the battle. It contained a five-dollar bill, a twenty, four ones, and a folded bit of paper which set his blood racing.

It was about the size of a playing card, perforated with dozens of tiny round holes, scattered like buckshot on a target. Their clean-cut edges indicated that they had been made tediously with a paper punch. He studied the strange patterns thoughtfully:

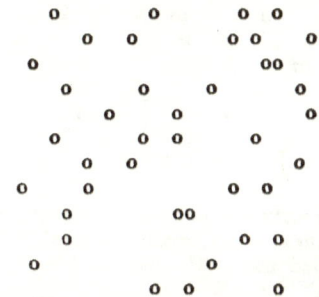

He observed that, scattered haphazardly though they appeared to be, the circles were arranged evenly in horizontal lines.

"The size of a playing card," Dunn muttered. "So was the opium message!"

The copy of the cryptogram he had painfully typed was in his pocket. He placed it alongside the perforated paper.

"That's it!" he cried. *"A lattice!"*

His fingers shaking, he placed the punched paper over the cryptogram. Through each tiny opening showed a single typed letter, as through a window!

But they made no sense as he spelled out the letters. His elation died. It was quite possible that there was a code within a code.

"Wait a minute—this thing can work four ways," Dunn muttered. "It has two sides, and a top and bottom."

He tried again, turning over the punched paper. The result was an unintelligible jumble. Perspiration began to ooze out on his brow. It was unthinkable that he could fail now when he was so near the answer!

He turned the paper around, tried once more, and choked off a cry of satisfaction. Letters leaped out at him as if written in fire:

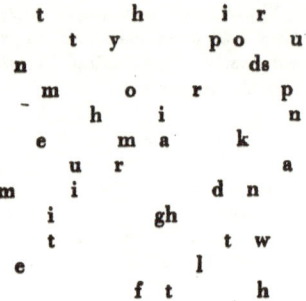

"Thirty — pounds — morphine — makura — midnight — twelfth," he spelled out. "By the Lord, we've got 'em!"

He turned feverishly to the shipping pages of a newspaper he had brought with him. There, among the routine notices of arrivals and departures, was the message he sought. "Makura arrives today via Sydney, Rarotonga and Papeete."

The twelfth — today was August twelfth! And at midnight the merchants of panic would smuggle off thirty pounds of a deadly narcotic—ammunition to keep their monstrous plot in operation for weeks! Provided, Dunn reflected, that Ko Fat Lu got the message of the tin in time.

"Clever devils!" he muttered, jaw set in a straight line. "They must have known the department would concentrate its attention on boats coming in from Honolulu, China and Japan. So they ship their dope through the South Seas via Australia!"

His job now, he realized grimly, was to get the opium tin to Ko Fat Lu. But the morphine shipment on the Makura had to be intercepted too. He could not call Bolstad—there had been too many leaks through his department. Well, there might be a way around that.

HE went out to a cigar store phone booth and called the *Morning Blade*.

"Managing Editor," he snapped. "Hello! Want to crack the Black Dragon story wide open? At midnight they'll try to smuggle thirty pounds of morphine off the Makura, just in from Papeete—"

He could almost see the managing editor choking on his excitement.

"Never mind who's talking," Dunn clipped out. "Go straight to D. J. headquarters and make sure their best men are covering the pier. Don't tip off the customs boys or you'll lose your story. Midnight—Makura. Got it?"

Dunn hung up, cutting off a blast of excited questions. Slipping out of the booth, he walked to another phone three blocks away, repeated his story to the editor of an evening paper. On his way back to the hotel he picked up a paper and bought a cheap wrist watch.

Lying on his bed, he scanned the headlines:

DRAGON RIOTS SPREAD PANIC

Hysterical Mobs Battle Police—Financial Structure Shaken

Dunn crumpled the paper savagely. It was noon now. Another three hours and the banks would close for the day. They could weather a one-day run, but if it kept up for another twenty-four hours — Dunn's face was drawn, his eyes burning as he considered the consequences. And if there was to be heartening news in the morning, it all depended on one man—Drover Dunn.

Why, he wondered, had the Chinese in the black sedan been carrying the lattice that decoded that all-important message? He could be no more than a hired thug of Ko Fat Lu. Something about the incident failed to ring true, but the answer eluded him maddeningly. Dunn had the tantalizing feeling that the solution to the whole perplexing problem danced elusively just beyond his reach.

He gave it up presently, settled down for a short nap, and awoke promptly at seven. He freshened up, had a meal sent up to him, and when he had finished went about his preparations for his rendezvous with death.

The gun was in its shoulder sheath, the opium tin in his inner coat pocket. In the bathroom cabinet he found a roll of adhesive tape. Stripping off his shirt, he taped the Black Dragon knife beneath his left armpit. The tip of the blade nearly reached his elbow, but the shirt sleeve concealed it.

At eighty-thirty he took the elevator to the lobby, walked through it briskly and caught a street car to the Embarcadero. The night was bracing with the chill that August sometimes brings to San Francisco. He walked the rest of the distance to the Ferry Building, lost himself in the throngs inside.

Promptly at nine he sauntered through the main entrance to the street. In hurrying crowd of pedestrians he could distinguish no one who evinced the slightest interest in him. He didn't expect to. Leisurely he began to saunter up Market Street.

He had covered half a dozen blocks when he observed a green sedan crawling out of the traffic line toward the curb. Then everything happened at once. Dunn found himself suddenly between two men who had walked up from behind him. They were both Chinese.

He snarled a warning, made an abortive movement toward his gun. His fingers dropped helplessly as the man at his right jabbed something hard and ominous through his pocket into Dunn's side.

"Please — you get into car." The soft words of the Chinese were belied by the baleful glitter of his eyes. "Have gun in pocket—not like to shoot."

Dunn hesitated, as if meditating a break. He mustn't let them think he was surrendering too easily. Then he shrugged, stepped toward the car.

The net was closing. Haig had played his part! The ruse had worked!

CHAPTER VI

The Yellow Robe of Ko Fat Lu

DUNN pitched into the rear seat with a captor on either side. The motor purred, headed up Market Street. Fingers ran over his clothing, came away with his gun and the tin of opium.

"Velly good." The Chinese at his left made a little cluck of satisfaction. "Now, please, we blindfold. You fight, get knocked on head."

Dunn had expected something of the sort. His last glimpse out of the rear window burned a lasting picture in his mind. Somewhere among those hurrying pedestrians, the string of cars, friendly eyes would be following him.

He was forced to crouch uncomfortably on the floor as a silken scarf was wrapped around his face. He tried to register the twists and turns of the car in his memory, but soon gave it up as hopeless. For at least thirty minutes the car droned on steadily. They might have been ten miles away, or within a block of the spot where they picked Dunn up.

He was pushed out of the car finally, and suffered himself to be led blindly. They were going down a flight of steps. A strange, dank mixture of subterranean scents assailed him. The scarf was whipped from his eyes and he found himself standing in an ill-lit passageway. A dark doorway yawned to his right.

"We come back soon." There was no expression on the yellow face. The Chinese was holding the opium tin. They would be in a hurry to translate the note it concealed, he knew. But that suited the G-man—he had planned on that.

A vicious shove on the back propelled him through the doorway. He heard the door slam shut and a bolt drop in place. In the throbbing darkness he growled under his breath, "Lousy devils!"

"Who—who's there?" A high-pitched voice quavered out of the blackness.

Startled, Dunn fumbled for a packet of matches in his pocket and struck one. The flickering flame etched a cringing, emaciated figure huddled in a corner. Two glaring eyes stared at the G-man from a blob of a pinched white face. The man's bony fingers clawed and twitched. His body was wracked by convulsive spasms.

"Hophead!" Dunn breathed. He touched the dying match to a stubby candle sticking in a bottle on a table. The light showed him a small, bare room, a bed covered with dirty rags, a table littered with unwashed dishes and remnants of food.

"Get up!" Dunn growled. He looked at his wrist watch. It was five minutes of ten.

The man dragged himself to his feet, stared wild-eyed at Dunn, and after a moment burst into a screaming laugh which shivered along Dunn's spine.

"So Ko Fat Lu got you too! How do you like it—knowing that in a few minutes you've got to die, die, *die!*"

That shrieking cry rasped Dunn's nerves raw. The man was wild for a shot of dope; going to pieces. Dunn handed him a cigarette. The man's hand trembled like a leaf in a breeze as he lit it in the candle flame. But it quieted him somewhat.

"What makes you think we're going to die?" Dunn asked.

"Nobody enters the headquarters of the Black Dragons and lives to tell about it. This waiting is driving me mad. Glad you've come . . . Somebody to talk to. I tried to double-cross Ko Fat Lu. Tipped off another Chink to an opium shipment the Dragons had coming in. I was to get a couple of pounds of morphine all for myself. I'd

have sold my soul for that. I guess I did. Ko Fat Lu got wise." Two eyes like burning coals stared hauntingly at Dunn. "Who—who are you? What have you done?"

Dunn grinned mirthlessly. "I knew the Chink you sold out to—Ching Hong."

"You—*knew him?*"

The G-man nodded. "He knocked off that opium shipment. I got a can of the stuff from him just before the dragons rubbed him out."

AN animal-like moan of pain bubbled from the man's lips. He jerked to his feet, staring, wildly, then subsided.

"They got him—and we're next! That devil will—"

"You mean Ko Fat Lu?" Dunn rapped out. "Tell me—what's he like?"

"A monster! A devil! I've never seen him. I didn't know until tonight that I'd been running with the Black Dragons. I was on the outside—doing dirty work; picking up smuggled shipments; peddling stuff. Jobs where I might get picked up by the cops. No, I don't know much about the devils. They took good care I shouldn't—"

He was going to pieces again. Dunn gave him the rest of his cigarettes.

"Why not tell me all about it?" Dunn asked soothingly. "How'd you get into the racket? How does the gang operate?"

The man's bloodless lips parted in a leer that gave Dunn the jitters.

"You wouldn't believe that three years ago my name meant something. John Faucette. Ever heard it? Respected, successful business man. It's—kind of funny. I was a bank cashier—"

Dunn's whole body tensed. "*Bank cashier?*" he shot out.

"Yes. Lumbermen's National. I started hitting the dope after an accident that tore me apart inside. I got the habit. It was expensive and finally drove me to dipping into the bank's funds; covering up in my books. I was into them for twelve thousand before the explosion came."

"This was three years ago?" Dunn's voice was savage, deadly. The shock of his staccato words smashed into Faucette like gun slugs, bewildered him. "Think!" said the G-man, "You confessed *three years ago?* What happened then?"

"They fired me. No publicity. Afraid of the effect on the bank—" Faucette's voice rose in a scream. "Don't look at me like that! I'm telling you the truth—"

Dunn swerved his glance away from the man, staring unseeingly at a blank wall. The muscles of his jaw twitched, and his smile, bitter and sardonic, was an accusing thing turned inward upon himself. A damp film of moisture oozed out on his brow and his burning stare was terrible with self-mockery.

He looked at his watch again. The hands were crawling toward ten-thirty. He paced the room like a caged beast. He had missed just one tiny trick in his mad gamble, but that one trick was going to cost him his life, smash the house of cards he had carefully erected.

"There's still a chance—one chance," he breathed. "God help me if it doesn't work!"

A gust of air eddied past Dunn's cheek and the candle flame flickered. He wheeled abruptly as a scream of terror froze on Faucette's lips.

The door had opened soundlessly. Four huge, evil-visaged yellow men, stripped to the waist, padded in. Outside the doorway stood two figures swathed from head to toe in yellow silken robes. Only their eyes were visible through the masking hoods. Guns dangled from hands below wide yellow sleeves.

There was no order, no command. Two of the Orientals ranged themselves alongside Faucette, herded him toward the door. The remaining pair fell in beside Dunn. He drew himself up and marched out into the dim passage with his sinister escort. His eyes missed nothing.

The passageway ended abruptly in a stout oaken door. There was a bolt on the outside and another within, Dunn noticed as he stepped over the threshold. Then his thoughts were swept away as he stared into the room ahead of him.

It was a chamber some thirty feet long, almost square. Luxurious embroidered silks hung from all four walls. There was a long table in the center of the room, surrounded with upholstered chairs. Ranged about the room, arms folded ominously, were a dozen yellow-robed figures.

But Dunn hardly spared a glance for them. His eyes were fixed on a dais at the extreme end of the room. Two figures sat there watching him impassively through the eye-slits of their yellow hoods. One of them, Dunn realized, must be the malevolent Ko Fat Lu. Who, then, was his companion? Dunn was bitterly confident that he could guess.

HIS guards led him before the dais. "The honorable Ko Fat Lu has deigned to summon you," said one.

From the robed figure at the right of the dais rolled an unctuous voice.

"The Black Dragons thank you, Drover Dunn, for the gift of the opium tin." The voice was droning, malignant, but with scarcely a trace of accent. "It contained, as you could not know, a message for us. Since you are so soon to embark on a long voyage, it may interest you to be acquainted with a quaint custom of the Dragon. The merchants who supply us the contraband we deal in, include with each shipment a message explaining where and when the next consignment will arrive. For reasons you can understand, it is really only *half* a message. To understand it a key—a lattice—is required."

Ko Fat Lu bowed slightly toward the motionless figure beside him.

"That explains the presence tonight of our honored leader. Unfortunately, in a struggle this morning, the lattice key to the message was lost. Happily our leader had a duplicate which he has just delivered, and you will be pleased to learn, Mr. Dunn, that our agents are at this moment on the way to obtain a shipment of thirty pounds of morphine."

Dunn glanced at his wrist watch. It was now nearly eleven. The officers who followed him should have burst into the den before this. He had told Haig to have them wait exactly one hour. The deadline was past.

"It happens that I had the tin in my pocket this morning when your thugs attacked me," Dunn grinned, sparring for time. "If you'd known that you wouldn't have been so damned careful to order them to take me alive, would you?"

The figure at Ko Fat Lu's right stiffened.

"It cannot matter now," Ko Fat Lu purred. "Our council has gathered to hear from your own lips, Mr. Dunn, exactly what your government knows about us. We were not aware until today that the phantom Federal agent— yourself, of course — was interested in us."

"No?" Dunn rasped. "Then why did you toss a knife at me last night?"

The yellow hood moved in a negative head shake.

"The Black Dragons threw no knife. If we had, we would not have missed."

"Then it was your pal Ching Hong, after all," Dunn said. "Clever devil. Figured I'd listen to him, I suppose, if I thought the Dragons knew me—"

Ko Fat Lu clapped his hands together.

"The affair of Ching Hong was unfortunate," he murmured. "We will take a few moments to show you how he died—and to convince you of the advisability of answering the questions we will shortly put to you."

Faucette screamed as his guards hurled him to the table top, spread-eagled him there with silken cords lashing down his hands and feet. Sweat poured out of Dunn's pores as he watched. He started to leap toward the table, thought better of it as his own guards closed in.

Fascinated, he watched one of the robed figures step forward and drop a cellophane sack over Faucette's stricken face. Faucette was beyond screaming now, as if death had already swept down horribly upon him. His features were ghastly beneath the transparent envelope, which formed an almost airtight covering.

Another robed Chinese stepped up, holding a length of narrow rubber tubing. He pinched the lower end together, and from a spill of rice paper carefully poured a powdery substance into the open end. An icy chill crept up Dunn's spine as he watched the man slit an opening in the top of the cellophane bag and insert the end of the tube through it.

"Powdered cobra venom," Ko Fat Lu was purring. "It acts rather more swiftly than an actual snake bite, as we have developed it. The particles, drawn into the lungs, spread swiftly to the blood stream—"

A muffled cry moaned from Faucette's lips. The Chinese bent over him, pursed his lips to the end of the tube, exhaled a sudden breath. A fine white mist moved in swirls and clouds within the cellophane envelope. Dunn closed his eyes to shut out Faucette's convulsive agony. A picture flashed through his mind of Ching Hong seated in the chair in that grimy little hotel room, a deadly mist pouring through a gas tube, spreading poison on the air. A mist which had given Dunn a splitting headache and an attack of nausea when he had entered the room later before it had settled.

IN the taut silence the blood pounded maddeningly at Dunn's ears. He wheeled about, shutting out the sight of the torture he was helpless to prevent.

"You're riding to a fall, Fat Lu," he shouted. "Damn your yellow soul to hell! You killed Blanchard, too, the same way—"

"Ah, yes, Blanchard!" Ko Fat Lu stiffened. "Unfortunately, he came to know too much about our operations. He actually suspected the location of the bank vault in which we keep the names of our—customers. The gentlemen who, in exchange for morphine, are kind enough to dip their fingers into the treasuries of their employers—"

He broke off suddenly as the sound of excited voices at the outer door drifted in. Dunn turned to face it, saw that every robed figure was staring at the entrance. He rested his hands across his breast, fingers under his armpits, waiting.

Through the door burst a disheveled C h i n e s e. Blood was caked in his oily hair around a flesh wound in the temple. He stumbled toward the dais, bowed, almost fell.

"Federal agents—watch Makura!" he g a s p e d. "Catch morphine—shoot three our men—capture all rest except me!"

The man collapsed in a heap. Ko Fat Lu was on his feet, muttering oaths in Cantonese. The robed figure beside him stood up like a puppet jerked by a string. Panic had touched the mob. In the excitement Dunn edged closer to the dais. For a moment, stricken by this new development, no one was paying any attention to him.

His fingers had been fumbling beneath his coat, through his shirt front. He leaped with the speed of an uncoiled spring, and the knife of the Black Dragon flashed out from his armpit and came to rest with its tip square against the breast of Ko Fat Lu's companion.

"One move and I'll cut your heart out!" Dunn gritted. "You, Fat Lu— get back!" The sharp command rasped out with the ring of steel. Ko Fat Lu oozed backward, fumbling in his robe. "If anyone shows a gun I'll sink this

blade. If anybody shoots, I'll drive it in before I drop! Tell 'em that—and make it stick!"

"Don't shoot!" Dunn's victim yelled. It was a white man's voice, sharp-edged with terror. "Do as he says—do you hear me?"

They were still twenty feet from the door, and yellow figures edged in to block the way. Dunn's left arm snaked out, circled his victim's neck, whirled him around. The knife pricked him under the shoulder blade.

"March!" snapped the G-man. "To the door—and if you want to live see that your men keep clear."

"Don't try to stop him!" screamed the hooded man. "He can't get away—watch your chance!"

The robed figures parted grudgingly. Dunn tightened his strangle hold, prodded with the knife, drew a scream of pain. It had all happened in a swift instant. Another moment and they would recover from their surprise. He pushed his advantage, raced toward the door, covered by his captive. He was afraid of the passageway, of connecting tunnels which might cut him off from the outside.

As they reached the door a babble of Cantonese broke out behind them. The Black Dragons were organizing their counter attack.

Dunn slammed the door behind him, dropped the bolt. The oak shivered under the shock of bodies hurled against it. The devils, he knew, would be pouring through another exit in a moment.

His elbow tightened around the man's neck and brought a strangled gurgle. Dunn's muscles tightened like steel cables, and his constricting arm half lifted the man from his feet. Like a football player charging a dummy, he raced down the dim passage with the roar of angry voices dimming in his ears.

He was aware that his knife was lashing at the yellow robe, ripping it to shreds. His victim kicked and struggled. A heel came up, caught Dunn in the groin. Paralyzing pain stabbed through him. He doubled over and the two went down in a heap. The knife flew from Dunn's fingers.

He gritted his teeth, smashed a fist at the yellow hood, dragged the man up and started on. His mind was foggy now. The pain of the kick maddened him, and his eyes were curtained by a red mist. Savagely his fists lashed out at the dim yellow figure, crashed into bone and muscle with berserk fury. The man backed away, screaming, stumbled on the bottom step of a flight of stairs.

DUNN'S brain began to clear. He twisted a robed arm behind the man's back, bent it upward remorselessly. Something snapped. A shriek of agony ripped from the man's lips. Dunn had him by the throat again, dragging him up the steps. The clamor was renewed from the Dragons' den. He thought he heard the crash of splintered timbers.

His labored lungs sucked in draughts of chill night air. He was outside now, in a dark alley. Far ahead loomed the lights of a distant street.

With a wild scream his captive broke away, raced from the alley.

"That's right—head for the street, damn you!" Dunn's gasping cry was a savage yell of elation. In his fury he was a fighting man gone mad, thrilling to the crush of flesh and bone beneath his flailing fists.

They had reached the street now. Dunn had a vague sensation that people were closing in on them, yelling. Before him the man in the yellow robe swayed and staggered, one arm hanging limp. Mercilessly Dunn's fist crashed home on his jaw. The man sagged, went to his knees, dropped face down.

Someone was tugging at Dunn's arm. He wheeled fiercely, braked his blow in mid-swing.

"Bolstad!" he cried. The fog was dissipating from his brain. He saw a half dozen square-shouldered figures rushing up behind the inspector. "Back down this alley—about midway—door leading to a cellar. Dragons' den—*hurry!* Ko Fat Lu—"

A police whistle skirled in the night. Figures pounded down the alley, guns flashing in steady hands as they ran.

"Dunn!" Bolstad gasped. "I was afraid they'd picked you off. Been combing Chinatown for you." He knelt beside the moaning figure in the robe, staring at the ashen face revealed through the torn fragments of the yellow hood. "They've broken his arm! Good God, man, I had no idea they'd got *him* too! Thank the Lord you saved him!"

"I didn't exactly save him," said Dunn caustically. "He happens to be your Black Dragon, Bolstad, all wrapped up and delivered."

Bolstad leaped to his feet, stared incredulously, tried to speak but could find no words. Dunn leaned down and ripped away the shreds of the yellow robe.

The stricken face which stared up at him was that of Robert Haig.

IN Bolstad's office, two hours later, Dunn sat smoking a cigarette and regarding his superior with a smile of sardonic amusement.

"We found everything in Haig's safety deposit vault, just as you expected," Bolstad was saying. "The names of every business employee the ring had under its thumb. And the boys cleaned up every yellow devil in that cellar. With Faucette's body lying there we can get 'em all on a murder rap. You've broken the back of the Black Dragon, Dunn. But how you did it is more than I can figure—"

"Luck," said Dunn laconically. "I'm really a triple-plated fool, Bolstad. If I'd had a nickel's worth of brains I'd have guessed this morning. I had a feeling there was something funny about one of those Chinks dropping a billfold containing the lattice. It never occurred to me then that it had been lost by *Haig*."

He lit a cigarette and blew smoke through his nostrils.

"When that poor devil Faucette told me he'd gone on the dope three years ago and the president of the Lumbermen's National Bank knew it, I began to put two and two together. That was quite a while before the Dragons began operations. I figure that Haig was a high-liver and needed dough. Faucette's embezzlements probably gave him the idea for looting banks wholesale and still keeping his own skin in the clear. Haig's friend, Blanchard, must have suspected something—so he died. Just a guess, Bolstad, but you can sweat it out of Haig."

"Don't worry," said Bolstad grimly. "We have. Ko Fat Lu wasn't much help to us. He didn't know Haig's identity. Neither did other members of the ring. That was the idea behind those fantastic yellow robes."

Bolstad fumbled in a drawer of his desk and produced a yellow paper.

"Thought you'd be interested in copies of these wires," he said dryly. "I've been checking up at Washington. It was Haig, through a front man, who got through that order for your suspension. He was afraid of the phantom Federal agent whose face none of his gang had ever seen. So he took a short cut and got you fired. You might be interested to know that you're back in the service, with a few citations."

"I suspected it," said Dunn dryly.

Bolstad's glance was just a bit malicious. "I still don't understand why you tipped the D. J. boys off to that Makura shipment. They did a crack job—picked off the whole smuggling crew. But it was really a job that belonged to my department."

"Sometimes, Bolstad," Dunn answered softly, "a man makes mistakes. Chalk that one up to me."

"As you say." Bolstad got up wearily. He looked tired, careworn. "I wish to hell you'd do your own publicity work sometimes, Dunn. It's a damned nuisance the way you keep under cover. I'm a wreck after breaking the story to that wild-eyed bunch of reporters. It had to be done, though. When the morning papers come out there'll be no more riots or runs on banks, thank God."

With meticulous care Bolstad restored his telegram copies to the drawer.

"Thirty minutes sleep in twenty-four hours," he grumbled. "I'm all shot. My nerves are crying for sleep. What do you say we go find ourselves a hot cup of coffee and a bed?"

"Why not?" said Drover Dunn.

Mail This Coupon Today!

The Silver Secret

Alone Can Save the Angel From the Chair

Gripping Moon Man Novelette

By FREDERICK C. DAVIS

Author of
"Moon Wizard," "Blood on the Moon," etc.

The Moon Man eased into the room of death

The Moon Man in trying to help his friend—the Angel—had thrust him into the sinister shadow of the electric chair. The Moon Man had the choice of letting his friend burn, or of unmasking himself. And in his frantic efforts the Moon Man discovered a crooked cop—whom he could never expose.

CHAPTER I

THE TENEMENT TERROR

THE man with the broken nose walked silently down the dark hallway. In an inside pocket he carried three hundred dollars in banknotes. The money was neatly packeted together by a band of silver paper. It had been stolen.

Ned Dargan, ex-pug, paused by a dark door. Farther down the hallway he saw another man pausing in front of another door. The other man's back was turned. A key rattled in the lock, and the other door opened. In a moment he was inside and gone.

Ned Dargan, sure now that he would not be seen, raised his hand to knock on the greasy panel of the door by which he had stopped. He never knocked.

A strangled cry echoed suddenly through the evil air of the old tenement. It came without warning—a wordless, toneless cry of terror. The next moment the gloomy silence that filled the place blotted it out.

At the first gasping sound, Ned Dargan twisted about, tensed. He stared at the door in the rear—the door through which the other man had just disappeared. It had come from there—that choking cry. He strode toward it. There was no sound now.

Dargan spoke to the door. He asked it: "Anything wrong?" The door did not answer.

Dargan laid his hand on the knob and twisted it. The door was unlocked. He pushed it open. Just over the sill, he stopped short.

A man was lying on the bed in the corner, squirming frantically. Around his head was a shapeless mass of white—soft, white stuff bunched about the shoulders. Desperately the hands of the man on the bed were clawing at it, trying to pull it away; but it would not come.

From within the mass of white which enveloped the struggling man's head came a horrible, breathless gasping sound.

Dargan stepped quickly into the room. It was a gloomy, sordid cell, typical of the impoverished tenement and the squalid neighborhood;

and now Dargan smelled death in the air. One window opened through the rear wall; it was closed. At the side of the bed Dargan stopped, staring at the white thing about the other man's head, staring at the frantic, clawing hands.

Dargan did not see a movement behind him. He did not see a man glide out of the triangular space behind the open door. He did not see that man slip close behind him, raising a hand which gripped an automatic by the barrel.

The heavy gun hissed through the air and crushed through the felt of Dargan's hat. A sharp, cracking sound resulted.

Dargan, being an ex-pug, made a half-completed left-hook as he dropped. He hit the edge of the bed, rolled off, and fell on his back with a loud thump. He did not even glimpse the man who had slugged him. It was a K.O. His last conscious thought was: *murder!*

IT was early evening. The tenement which Dargan had entered lay, queerly enough, not far from the downtown section which now glittered with lights. Auto horns blared; the air shook with noise. On a street corner a newsboy howled: "Re-ad about the lat-est robb'ry of the Moon Man!"

A few blocks farther on, in a quieter district again, sat Police Headquarters. It was aglow with lights. Behind the building ran a dark alleyway. Back to back with Headquarters, not twenty feet away, sat a boxlike brick structure, all black and empty. On the large double door in its rear wall was a sign: GARAGE TO LEASE

It looked deserted. It was not deserted. Inside was a presence.

Behind the double doors was dark hollowness. In one corner was a partitioned space which once had served as an office. The grimy window which opened into it was covered. The merest glow of light came from a dim yellow bulb high overhead.

A figure was standing in that small space. It was grotesque, black and shapeless, made so by a long cloak which hung from the broad shoulders of the man wearing the garment. Above the shoulders it was still more grotesque.

Its head was a round ball of silver, mottled with black markings, like the moon. It had no eyes, but the head turned as if looking around. It had no ears, but the head tilted as if listening for an approach. It had no mouth, but a muffled word came out of the silvery sphere: "Late."

Faintly from the street came the shrill cry of a newsboy: "Moon Man robb'ry!"

In the gloomy office of the deserted garage across the alley from Police Headquarters, the black figure chuckled softly. He was the Moon Man!

"Master thief" he was called. His daring exploits had electrified the city. He stole and went uncaught. All the desperate efforts of the police to catch him had failed. To the police it did not matter that the Moon Man stole only from those who deserved to lose ill-gotten gains: they wanted him badly.

The police did not know that the Moon Man never kept a cent of his loot for himself, but distributed it all to the poverty-ridden, whose very existence depended upon such help: it would have made no difference to them. And the police did not realize that the Moon Man's rendezvous was located within hailing distance of the office of the chief of police! . . . .

The Moon Man waited. Abruptly he turned. From a pile of worn tires in the corner he extricated a telephone. He spoke softly into the transmitter—the number of a very private line. He waited again while connection was made and the distant phone rang. There was no answer.

"Angel!" the Moon Man called impatiently.

There was no answer. And for a good reason. "Angel" was the Moon Man's secret ambassador, who distributed the loot to the poor. "Angel" was the Moon Man's affectionate nickname for one otherwise known as Ned Dargan.

Blocks away, all unknown to the Moon Man, Ned Dargan was lying unconscious in an odorous tenement room . . . .

The Moon Man replaced the telephone. He turned again quickly and made quick motions of his arms. First he divested himself of the globular, silver mask—a sphere of Argus glass, through which he could see clearly, while it hid his features behind the gloss of a mirror. He shook off his robe, slipped off his black gloves. His regalia he stored away quickly in a small safe in a corner; and he spun the combination. He was leaving his rendezvous . . . .

He slipped to a narrow door, inched it open, peered out, stepped through. Quickly he walked along the black alleyway. When he reached the street he turned; then he turned again, toward the bright entrance of Police Headquarters.

When the light fell upon him it disclosed the clean-cut features of Stephen Thatcher, Detective Sergeant, son of Peter Thatcher, chief of police!

STEVE THATCHER briskly climbed the steps to the second floor and opened the chief's door. Three men were inside. Behind the desk sat Chief Thatcher, portly, kind-faced, white-haired. Beside him was a grim-faced, hard-eyed detective: Gilbert McEwen. At Gil McEwen's side the third man was standing: Sidney McEwen, Gil's brother. They looked up as the door opened.

"Evening, son," said the chief.
"Hello, Steve," said Gil McEwen.
"Harya," said Sid McEwen.
"You look," said Steve Thatcher, "like serious business."

Gil McEwen was the ace sleuth of the force. A born man-hunter, merciless, relentless. He had been known to go to the far ends of the earth to get his man. No crook had succeeded in escaping him — save one. That one was the Moon Man.

He pointed vehemently at a photograph he was holding.

"I still swear to heaven that *this* is going to send the Moon Man up the river on so many counts of burglary that he'll never live to come out of the jug!"

Steve Thatcher shuddered and looked at the photograph. It was a picture of a door-knob, and on the door-knob was a clearly defined thumb-print. It was the only clue McEwen had ever found to the identity of the mysterious Moon Man. It was the Moon Man's own print—and Steve Thatcher's!

"I'm going to get that guy!" McEwen swore. "He can't get away with it forever! I'll get him!"

The telephone rang shrilly. Chief Thatcher picked it up and grumbled into the transmitter. Steve Thatcher meditatively rubbed the ball of his right thumb while his hand rested in his pocket.

If McEwen did some day "get him"? Discover the Moon Man to be the son of the chief of police? Learn that the Moon Man was in reality Steve Thatcher, who was engaged to marry Sue McEwen, his own daughter? The mere thought sent a chill of dread through Steve Thatcher.

The chief replaced the telephone and spun about.

"Gil, something's up at the tenement at 60 Spruce Street. Woman named Kaplin, first floor, says there's trouble. That's not far from where the Moon Man's old hangout was. Better take it!"

Gil McEwen's eyes glittered. "Right! I'll take it! I'm taking anything and everything that might lead to the Moon Man!"

He hurried from his chair to the door, followed by his brother, Sid McEwen. Steve Thatcher paused, still chilled, uncertain. Suddenly he hurried after them. Gil McEwen was no more anxious about the discovery of the Moon Man than he!

THE police car whizzed to a stop in front of the tenement. Gil McEwen and Sid McEwen and Steve Thatcher scrambled out of it. They marched into the tenement and halfway down the hall. Gil McEwen knocked loudly at a door.

The door opened and a haggish head appeared. "You phone headquarters, lady?"

"Yeh. Next door. Somethin's been goin' on next door. It sounded like a fight. There's nobody there now and the door's locked, but you'd better see. You never can tell what'll happen around here."

"Is that all you know about it? Who lives there?"

"Gen'man name Day. Do' know nothin' else."

McEwen marched to the next door toward the rear. It was, as the witch had said, locked, Hammering fists on it brought no response. McEwen drew back, looked at Steve Thatcher.

"Let's bust it," he said.

In three minutes it was busted. Steve Thatcher applied his shoulder to the panels of the door three times, heavily. They were football-playing shoulders. The door panel turned into kindling wood.

McEwen, in first, stopped short. The others crowded behind him.

On the floor was a young man with a broken nose; he was writhing, struggling to get up. Ned Dargan looked a little the worse for wear. A large lump undulated across his scalp. He wasn't sure yet what was going on.

McEwen was. "Grab that guy!" he ordered.

Sid McEwen grabbed that guy.

Steve Thatcher was staring. "Angel!" It almost burst through his lips—but he kept it back.

McEwen bent over the form on the bed. He couldn't make it out—the white mass wadded about the head of the man who lay there. The man was motionless, clawed hands gripping the soft white stuff that hid his face.

"Suffocated to death!" McEwen blurted. "What the hell?"

"Look at that — rusty metal," Steve Thatcher pointed out.

McEwen pawed, discovered that the white stuff was two wadded pillows and that, embedded deep in them, were two huge iron claws bearing together with terrific pressure. McEwen tried to pull them out: useless!

"I'll be damned! This thing is a big trap—probably a bear trap! It was hidden under the two pillows. When this man lay down, or was thrown down, the pressure of his head on the pillow sprang the trap. It closed over his head—choked him to death. By damn, that's nasty!"

Steve Thatcher glanced anxiously at Dargan. Dargan was sitting up, blinking. He did not recognize Steve Thatcher. He had never seen the face of the man he served as emissary—he did not know what the Moon Man looked like. The mask of Argus glass had done that. And so he did not know that the Moon Man, at that very moment, was in the room with him . . . .

"Let's get this thing off!" McEwen said.

Steve Thatcher helped pry the big trap off. It was not an easy job. They were able to slip it off the head of the man on the bed, and to pull the pillows from it. When they released it, its powerful springs snapped the toothed jaws together with a vicious click. McEwen was

hard-boiled; but when he peered at the man on the bed again he shuddered.

The features of the dead man were distorted, blackened. He had strangled slowly, horribly tortured. The brutal pressure of the trap jaws had punished him terribly, even through the padding of the pillows. McEwen stooped for a closer look.

"By damn!" he exclaimed. "Beekin!"

Sid McEwen, who was keeping a firm grip on Dargan, turned quickly. "Beekin?" he asked.

Steve Thatcher repeated: "Beekin?"

"Beekin!" exploded Gil McEwen. "I'll be double-damned! What do you think of *that!*"

They didn't say!

"What the hell is an ex-district attorney doing in this rat-hole?" McEwen demanded. "He couldn't be living in a place like this—not with all the money he's got! But listen—there's something damned odd about this. Beekin has been keeping out of sight for months!"

Four years ago Bradley Beekin had been receiving praise for ardent, honest work before the judiciary. In the latest election the machine had crushed him, thrown him out. Since passing from public life, little had been seen or heard of him. Still less would be seen and heard of him now!

"Murdered, all right!" Gil McEwen exclaimed. He turned swiftly on Dargan. "Yeah!"

Dargan swallowed hard. "God, my head hurts!" he remarked.

"A lot more of you is going to hurt a lot worse," Gil McEwen declared ominously, "if you don't start talking pretty quick. D'you rig up that trap to kill Beekin?"

"What trap?" asked Dargan.

"Don't give me any of that! Come on—talk!" McEwen snarled it.

Dargan said "Ow!" and held his head. But he began to talk. "I was coming down the hallway when I heard somebody yell. I opened this door and saw that guy on the bed. All at once somebody socked me on the head from behind—that's all I know."

"Yeah? Why'd you come into this place, anyhow?"

Steve Thatcher watched Dargan's face keenly. He knew the answer to that one. It was: "To distribute money stolen by the Moon Man." But Dargan didn't say that. Instead he answered:

"I just—came in."

Gil McEwen retorted: "Aw, hell! You're going to be one of these innocent guys, are you? Well, it looks like you did it yourself— killed Beekin! You're coming to headquarters with me and tell me so!"

Steve Thatcher tapped Gil McEwen's arm in sudden panic. "Wait a minute, Gil. The door was locked. A murderer wouldn't lock himself in the room with the man he killed."

"I guess this bird'll explain that along with a lot of other things!" McEwen snapped. "I'm not wasting time. I'm getting the fingerprint expert down here quick, and taking this guy to headquarters. You— come on!"

Suddenly the door-knob rattled. The four men turned quickly as the door began to open.

A girl stood just outside, staring in, terrified.

CHAPTER II

STOLEN LOOT

"WHAT—what's happened?" She was a very pretty girl. She was in her early twenties, trimly dressed, smart, enticing. She asked the question falteringly.

McEwen said quickly: "You're Barbara Beekin, aren't you? Bradley Beekin's daughter?"

"Yes."

"Stay right where you are!"

McEwen strode through the door and shut it, keeping the girl outside. Steve Thatcher frowned, peering at Dargan. He was thinking only of Dargan at the moment. It looked bad. Dargan found in the same room with a murdered man! What Gil McEwen wouldn't do with that!

Outside the door McEwen was talking softly to the girl. "Now, keep hold of yourself. Something's happened to your father — something pretty bad. Don't go to pieces."

The girl asked in a whisper: "Is he—dead?"

"Yes."

There was the sound of sudden, soft crying. McEwen spoke roughly. The sobbing stopped.

"I—I'll tell you," Barbara Beekin's voice came. "I was so afraid something would happen to father! He was, too—but he kept on—working—trying to find out."

"Find out what?"

The girl's voice became stronger. "You know that father was an excellent district attorney. He was honest. He couldn't be bought. It was for that reason he was broken by the political machine. He wouldn't give favors, wouldn't be bribed, so they got rid of him. It was heartbreaking—"

"Yeah, I know. Go ahead."

"Father was determined to crush the crooked political machine. He believed that Judge Benjamin is at the head of it. He came down here, took this room under the name of Day, and began mingling with the small fry of the machine, to learn the facts at first hand. I came to see him often; he wanted me to, though it was a risk—somebody might find out what he was doing. He was almost ready to act—he had all the facts he wanted—"

"What about 'em? Where's the dope he got?" McEwen asked quickly.

"He kept his notes in a cash box in the dresser."

The door opened suddenly as McEwen thrust in. He strode across the room, to the dresser, and jerked open its drawers one after another. In the bottom one he found a cash-box. He snapped open its lid and stared at—emptiness.

"Somebody swiped the stuff! That's why Beekin was killed! Somebody knew he had the dope on the political crooks and silenced him—and stole his notes!"

McEwen sidled out the door and rejoined the girl. "The stuff's gone," his voice came through.

"Oh! I was afraid—"

"Listen, Miss Beekin. You're taking this like a good soldier. Don't let go of yourself. I want you to come to headquarters with me and tell me all about it. I promise you I'll go to the ends of the earth to get the man who killed your father!"

The door jerked open again and McEwen stared in:

"Take that guy down with you, Sid. I'm going with Miss Beekin. Steve, stay here till Kenton arrives, then come along. Damn' nasty business!"

Sid McEwen took a tighter grip on Ned Dargan's arm. "Nasty as hell!" he growled. "Come on, you!"

He tugged Dargan through the door. Steve Thatcher heard Gil McEwen and the girl walking down the hallway. In a moment he was alone.

"Lord, Angel!" he exclaimed under his breath.

He peered at the dead man on the bed. Murdered in a room in which Ned Dargan had been found! Not for one moment did Steve Thatcher doubt Ned Dargan's innocence. Not for one moment could he blind himself to the fact that circumstances made it wretchedly black for Dargan—that at this very moment Dargan's steps were directed toward the electric chair! . . . .

"Lord, Angel!"

STEVE THATCHER hurried into police headquarters. He had remained in the sordid tenement room until Kenton, the fingerprint expert, had come and gone; until the medical examiner had done his work and departed. He hurried up the steps into the chief's office.

Gil McEwen and Sid McEwen were there.

"I thought so! I had a hunch!" Gil McEwen was exclaiming. "The Moon Man had a hand in it!"

Steve Thatcher stopped short. "The Moon Man?" he asked. "Had a hand in killing Beekin?"

Gil McEwen whirled on him. "Damn right! I've got proof! Kenton was just here, telling me what he found! The Moon Man's thumbprint on the door-knob again—and on the trap that killed Beekin!"

Steve Thatcher grew cold. "Sure of that, Gil?"

"Sure of it? Why shouldn't I be sure of it, and Kenton too? I know the Moon Man's fingerprint by heart! Every line of it is stamped right into my brain. We've got the knob and the trap here, and I've taken a look at 'em. It's the Moon Man's fingerprint, all right!"

Unconsciously Steve Thatcher thrust his right hand into his pocket. He could have explained that—explained how the Moon Man's fingerprint had appeared on the scene. Because Steve Thatcher had opened the tenement-room door with an ungloved hand! Because he'd helped release the deadly trap! But he didn't explain . . . .

"The print doesn't belong to—that chap we've got?" he asked quickly.

"No. He's not the Moon Man. But it's dollars to doughnuts that he's connected with the Moon Man somehow!"

"Did he say so?" Steve Thatcher asked the question quickly.

"No—he won't talk worth a damn!"

That was like Dargan. Faithful,

loyal, unquestioning. Steve Thatcher felt sure that all the third degrees in the world wouldn't make Dargan talk. Not even to save himself.

"What's the dope, Gil?" Steve Thatcher asked.

"Just as you heard it. Brad Beekin was broken by the political machine, thrown out. He's been hiding down in the slums, trying to find out who's the power in this town. Evidently he did. His daughter names Judge Benjamin, but she doesn't know any of the real facts her father found out. Beekin was killed to keep him quiet.

"The trap was set for him. I've got a hunch this bird we caught there did it. Maybe he was setting the trap when Beekin came in. There was a fight, and he threw Beekin on the bed—the trap did the rest. Maybe Beekin slammed him on the head, then fell on the bed. No matter. Dargan knows all about it. And so does the Moon Man!"

"What makes you think—"

"Because the Moon Man was there, in Beekin's room—he handled the trap! If he didn't engineer the killing himself, he's in with the gang that did!"

Steve Thatcher's heart was pounding. "What're you going to do about it, Gil?"

"Plenty! I've sent Miss Beekin home—she's upset. As for Dargan —I've got a plan. Listen."

McEwen stepped closer and spoke sibilantly.

"Dargan is tied up with the Moon Man—that's certain. He may know who the Moon Man is, where he hangs out—but he won't talk. All right — he won't have to talk. Actions speak louder than words!"

Sid McEwen asked: "What're you driving at, Gil?"

"If Dargan got loose, he'd probably lead us to the Moon Man. That's what I'm banking on! Sid, listen. I've got it planned out. Get Dargan and take him down to the first-aid room. It's just inside the front door. Tell him the doc's going to fix up his head. Then leave him alone there—get it? Leave him alone!"

Sid McEwen's eyes brightened; Steve Thatcher's filled with dread.

"You mean give him a chance to get away!" Sid McEwen gasped.

"Right! Give him a chance to get away. Let him walk out—beat it! He'll think he's escaping! He'll head for cover, and try to get in touch with his boss, sure as taxes! What do you think of that, Steve?"

STEVE THATCHER said grimly: "An excellent plan, Gil!"

"Right! Sid, go get Dargan right away. Start it working. I'll be on the watch!"

Sid McEwen eagerly hurried to the door and out it. Gil McEwen turned quickly, raised one of the chief's windows, and stood beside it.

"By damn!" he exclaimed. "This is the best stroke of luck I've had since I started after the Moon Man. It's a thousand to one that this'll get him!"

Steve Thatcher said thoughtfully, "Maybe you're right."

"The Moon Man's bigger game now than he once was, Steve! The fact that he's mixed up in this killing means that he's mixed up in the political machine that Beekin was investigating. God knows we're fighting terrific odds, trying to get anything on the machine—but this is our chance!"

Steve Thatcher nodded. "What can I do to help, Gil?"

"Sit tight! I'm handling this alone. I'm going to keep an eye on Dargan and shadow him!"

Suddenly the door opened. Sid McEwen hurried in.

"I left him in the first-aid room!" he exclaimed. "He's alone—and the door is open!"

"Great!"

Gil McEwen took his position beside the window. Keeping back, he could look down into the street outside. If Ned Dargan left headquarters, he would be seen! Steve Thatcher inwardly moaned.

"Angel! Don't take the bait!" he thought.

The room was silent.

Suddenly Gil McEwen turned back quickly. His eyes were glittering. "He's out!"

He retreated from the window quickly. Steve Thatcher glanced down at the street—just in time to see a black figure darting along the sidewalk, hurrying to the shelter of the alleyway.

"God, Angel!" he implored silently. "Stay away from the garage!"

Gil McEwen was snatching on his hat. "I'm on my way! That guy's going to lead me to the Moon Man!"

He slammed out the door. Steve Thatcher could hear him running down the stairway.

And Steve Thatcher's heart was a frozen thing . . . .

AN hour passed — silent, tense, long. Steve Thatcher paced back and forth across the office of the chief of police. He was alone. He was wondering . . . . So far no word from Gil McEwen . . . .

Suddenly he turned, strode out the office, ran down the stairs. He crossed the street to the corner cigar store and slipped into a phone booth. He called a number—the same very private number—and waited.

Soon a voice answered: "Angel!" Steve Thatcher said.

"Boss! Boss, I couldn't get to the garage tonight. I was—"

"I know, Angel! I know all about it. Listen—be careful! The cops are watching you. Right now Gil McEwen is watching you!"

"God, boss, how do you know all these things?"

"Never mind, Angel — but look out! McEwen gave you the chance to get away from headquarters—deliberately. He wants you to lead him to me."

"I thought of that, boss, so I

played safe. Don't worry — he'll never find out about you from me!"

"Bless you, Angel! Stay where you are—under cover."

"Right! Boss — Lord, I'm not mixed up in that murder. I don't know anything—"

"I know you don't, Angel—but you're in hot water. You'll go to the chair for it, probably, if the real murderer isn't caught."

"Gosh, boss—what'll I do?"

"Leave it to me, Angel. It's my job. You got into trouble working for me, and I've got to get you out of it."

"You, boss? With the cops looking for you? With McEwen red-hot on the trail? Boss, never mind about me—look out for yourself!"

"I'm looking out for you, Angel, chance or no chance. If I don't do it nobody else will. I'm going to get you out of this, no matter what the cost is!"

"Thanks, boss. Listen, boss. There's one funny thing. I went into that room, found that guy dying, and got slugged on the bean. But while I was knocked out, the money was stolen from me!"

"Stolen!"

"Yeah! I had the three hundred bucks you gave me to give to Mrs. Kaplin who lives in the next room. I never got a chance to give it to her. I was slugged and the money was taken from me and—boss, you got any idea who did it?"

"Who actually killed Beekin, Angel? Not any. I know what happened, though. The trap was set for Beekin when he walked in, surprising the man who was setting it. The murderer threw him on the bed. When you came in, he slugged you, robbed you, and beat it. I've got one small lead, Angel — just one. And I'm following that for all I'm worth. Sit tight!"

Steve Thatcher slipped out of the phone booth, crossed the street, and ducked into the alleyway. Making sure he wasn't watched, he slipped inside the garage. Five minutes later he came out again, carrying a small overnight case.

He walked into the headquarters garage, got into his roadster, and started it. The case was on the seat beside him. Right there in headquarters, all unknown, was the full regalia of the Moon Man—mask, cloak, gloves and all!

Steve Thatcher turned the car out of the door. As he started off he recalled the words spoken by Barbara Beekin in the unsavory tenement. One name stuck in his mind: *Judge Benjamin.*

Steve Thatcher stepped on the gas.

CHAPTER III

MOON MADNESS

JUDGE Victor Benjamin's huge house was located in a rich, quiet residential section. It was surrounded by spacious grounds; it bespoke wealth. This night a few windows on the upper floor of the house were shining brightly. The rest were black.

In the darkness that surrounded the mansion, a figure moved. It was vague, ghostlike—a shapeless black figure with a spherical head of silver! From out of the night the Moon Man materialized. The Moon Man's mission tonight was not one of robbery. It was a far grimmer game he was playing.

Under a window the Moon Man paused. He tested it. Locked. Deftly, through the slits in the sides of his cape, the Moon Man produced tools. A diamond glass-cutter. A small suction-cup on the end of a wooden rod. He worked quickly.

In a moment he had cut a half-circular section from the lower edge of the upper pane. He reached through and unfastened the catch. He raised the window. Silently he climbed in.

The Moon Man had judged well. He found himself in a luxuriously furnished study. It was walled with shelves, filled with a massive desk and chairs. And in one corner, set into the wall, was the flat, black front of a safe.

The Moon Man moved toward the safe. He knelt, deftly spun the combination-dial with black-gloved hands. His moon-shaped head turned slightly as he listened. The clicks he heard would have been inaudible to another man. But the Moon Man heard. And he knew locks. He swung open the door of the safe.

Quickly he searched through the compartments, the drawers. He was searching for papers—such papers as had been stolen from the room in which Beekin had died. Two swift minutes of hunting told him that the papers were not there.

Not there!

Suddenly a bell rang. It was far away in the house, but it brought a quick response. Footfalls began coming down a flight of carpeted stairs not far away. In the darkness the Moon Man turned, pressing himself against the wall. The footfalls were coming nearer now . . . .

A black shadow passed the open door of the study. It was a large, heavy-set man; he did not look in. He was answering the ring at the front door.

The Moon Man turned again. He slipped to the window through which he had entered. Silently he slid it up. Quickly he slipped through the opening. He dropped to the ground without a sound; but he did not move away. After lowering the window, he remained, crouched, listening.

In the gloom his silver head sparkled.

Suddenly light burst through the window above him. Sounds came from the study. The Moon Man knew that two men had entered it. Voices came.

"Well? Did you bring them?"

THE Moon Man knew that heavy, assured voice. It was that of Judge Victor Benjamin — man of wealth, political power, social position and prestige.

"I said, did you bring them?"

"What do you think? No, I didn't bring them. I'm no fool!"

The second voice was almost inaudible, scarcely more than a whisper. With a shock, the Moon Man recognized a familiar something in it—but he could not place it. He turned his silver head to hear more clearly.

"You did what I told you, didn't you?" Judge Benjamin demanded.

"I did, and damn' near got caught! I had it fixed when he walked in! I had to knock him down —throw him on the bed! And he yelled when I did it. Next thing I knew somebody was at the door. I had to do some more slugging—to get out."

"You blundered, did you? You didn't get the notes!"

"I got 'em, all right!"

"Well, then? What does anything else matter? Where are they?"

"Where they'll be safe, judge. Where you won't be able to get them without my say-so."

"What! I told you to bring them here! You fool—"

"Don't call me a fool! I know what I'm doing! You thought all you had to do was ask me to get those papers, and I'd do it! Well, you're dead wrong. I know what that stuff is worth to you. And, believe me, I'm going to collect."

A silent pause followed. The Moon Man did not move.

"I see," the judge's voice came coldly. "This is what is called blackmail."

"It's business, and nothing else! I ran the risk, getting that stuff! I had to kill a guy to get the papers you want! I'm not handing 'em over so easy! You're going to pay for 'em!"

"Yes? How much?"

"One hundred grand!"

"That's preposterous!"

"It's cheap at the price. You've got the money, and I've got you up a tree. You'll pay!"

Another pause.

"I see . . . . I'll think it over."

A short laugh answered the judge. "All right. But go easy, Judge. You can't do anything to me. You're in a hot spot—you wouldn't dare bump me off now, or afterward. If you did, you'd get the chair, and you know it! You'll come across, all right!"

"You're pretty clever, aren't you?"

"Clever enough to see my chance and take it! You know what's good for you! You'll buy the stuff from me and once you get it you won't dare touch me. I'm telling you that again. You wouldn't dare take the chance of bumping off a—"

"I'll think it over, I said. I'll phone you."

"Okay, judge. You know where to get me. The sooner the better. I want cash, small, old bills. You've got an account at the Day and Night National, and you can get it any time. I'll turn the stuff over to you when you turn the cash over to me. Every minute you wait is dangerous, judge. Good-night."

The Moon Man straightened. He heard footfalls in the room, moving away. Soon the front door of the house opened, unseen, and heels gritted in the gravel path. From the shadows the Moon Man could see a black figure moving toward a car parked at the curb.

A click came from the study. The Judge was picking up a telephone. In a moment his voice rasped:

"Hurst? Jake there? Okay? Good—get busy. Yes, just as I instructed you. The sooner the better. Right! And Hurst— No, that's all right. I've changed my mind. I've got another little job in mind, but I'll handle it myself. Good-night."

The Moon Man raised silently

and looked through the window. Judge Benjamin was opening a drawer of his desk. The judge lifted into view a huge, glittering automatic. He thrust it into his pocket, turned, and strode from the room.

QUICKLY the Moon Man divested himself of his cloak, his mask. The "public enemy" disappeared; the detective, Steve Thatcher, stood in his place. A few more quick movements, and the regalia of the Moon Man was stored in the overnight case.

Steve Thatcher walked quickly to the gate of the Benjamin estate. The car which had started away was running along the street. Thatcher hurried to the corner, to the spot where he had left his roadster, and hopped into it. The next moment he was rolling along the boulevard after the car of the man who had unknowingly confessed the killing of Bradley Beekin.

The other car led Steve Thatcher around the business district. Surprisingly, it turned into the street which ran past police headquarters. Still more surprisingly, he turned again, suddenly, and shot into the police garage!

Steve Thatcher's heart thumped heavily. He was still too far away to have learned who the driver of the other car was. He stepped on the gas, turned into the police garage, and braked to a stop.

He looked around; but he could not be sure which of the parked cars had just come in. He saw a mechanic in the rear of the garage and called quickly:

"Hey, Smitty! Who was it, just arrived?"

"Do' know, Steve. I just stepped in through the side door."

Steve Thatcher was deeply troubled. He locked the case in the rumble compartment of his roadster, then sidled into the headquarters building, and walked quickly up the stairs to the chief's office. A light was shining through the rippled glass; he pushed his way in.

Sid McEwen was sitting at the chief's desk, leisurely smoking a cigar.

"Hello, Sid," Steve said. "Any word from Gil?"

"Nope. He's on the job, watching Dargan. You know Gil. He won't let go."

"Right. Who's following up the girl's angle on this case? The dope she gave us about the crooked political machine?"

"I am."

"What's doing?"

"If you ask me," Sid McEwen said, "it's the toughest case anybody was ever asked to handle in this town. We all know that politics aren't what they should be. No political machine is absolutely straight. Well, there's plenty of crookedness in this town, too—only it's going to be hell, trying to prove it."

"It is anywhere. Look at Seabury in New York."

"Right. I think it's worse here, because we deal with persons rather than with organizations. Take Judge Benjamin, for instance. Everybody suspects he's crooked. But he's got money, and he's got power—plenty of pull. He could get us all thrown out on our ears if he wanted to—everybody from the chief on down. And if we got kicked out, we wouldn't be able to fight him, and he'd soon have his own chief of police in the place. I'm not kidding, Steve. Look at what happened to Beekin."

"You're right, Sid — but you're not letting it slide, are you?"

"Hell, no! There's murder involved. If we can find out who Beekin had the dope on, we'll know who killed him, or had him killed. It's my job to handle that end of it, and I'll do the best I can."

Sid McEwen was rolling a small wad of paper between his fingers pensively. He had taken it from his pocket while talking. He smiled at Steve.

"Boy, won't this be a blow-up when we crack the case! Gil's fully expecting to get the Moon Man, too, this time!"

"I know he is," Steve Thatcher said quietly.

Sid McEwen rose, y a w n e d, stretched—and tossed the wad of paper into the waste-basket.

"Well, so-long, Steve," he said.

Steve Thatcher nodded so-long. Sid McEwen went out. Steve rose, walked across the carpet, back again. His eye was attracted by a glint of light that came from the waste-basket. Curiously he stooped and picked up a small, tightly rolled ball. He unravelled it.

It was a broken band of silver paper! Identically the same kind of silver paper which always packeted the money given to Dargan for distribution by the Moon Man! Exactly the same kind of paper which had bundled the $300 stolen from Dargan in the death room!

"Good Lord!" Steve Thatcher gasped.

One little slip of silver paper, tossed absent-mindedly into a waste-basket—but it marked Sid McEwen as a murderer!

"STEVE, darling—hello!"

Steve Thatcher jerked about. He had not heard the door opening. But it was open now, and a girl was coming toward him. She was a very pretty girl. She was Sue McEwen.

She went into his arms. He kissed her briefly. She drew back, surprised. Her left hand rested on Steve Thatcher's shoulder, and on its third finger a diamond solitaire glittered. Steve had given her that. They were soon to be married . . . .

"Not very ardent, Steve," said Sue. "What's the matter?"

Steve Thatcher laughed brokenly. "Tired out, I guess. Working hard. I really am glad to see you, Sue."

"I dropped in just to see you, Steve," she smiled. "I know you've been going at it too hard. Now you must knock off. Let's drive home together."

"I'm sorry, Sue," Steve said quickly. "I can't do that. I—I've got an important job on tonight."

"Oh, Steve! I've seen you so little lately. Please come."

"I simply can't!"

Steve Thatcher turned toward the door, abruptly, unable to hide his uneasiness. S u d d e n l y the door opened again. Gil McEwen, red of face, tramped in heavily.

"Oh—Sue," he said. "Hello."

"Hello, dad. You look as tired as Steve. Both of you are working yourselves into nervous breakdowns trying to get the Moon Man. I don't think he's worth it!"

Steve winced. Gil McEwen eyed his daughter grimly.

"Nervous breakdown or not, I'm going to grab that guy before I'm through! I'm closer to it now than I ever was before! It's only a matter of time until I've thrown that crook into the jug!"

Again Steve Thatcher winced. "Any new dope on him, Gil?"

"No. I've got Wilson watching Dargan's room. He's going to phone me if Dargan leaves. I've got a new hunch on this case, and I've got to follow it. Now, Sue, you run along and let us alone."

Steve Thatcher grasped the opportunity. "Better do that, Sue. I'll see you tomorrow—that's a promise."

He hurried to the door and through it. Rapidly he ran down the stairs, not daring to look back. Once in the garage, he hopped into his roadster, started the engine, and swung out of the big door.

He sent the car whining along the street.

God, what an ordeal that had been! Having to face Sue and Gil McEwen immediately after finding proof that Sid McEwen was a thief and a murderer! Facing them with that knowledge—with the determination that the secret he knew must remain a secret.

The danger that Steve Thatcher would be discovered to be the Moon Man was a dreaded menace to him: but discovery of Sid McEwen's guilt by them would be as bad. Gil's own brother! Sue's uncle! Let them learn of it? Impossible! . . . .

Yet— Steve Thatcher thought of Ned Dargan. He had said to Dargan, "The only way of clearing you is to discover the real murderer." Unless that was done, Dargan was heading for a stretch up the river at the least—perhaps the chair! To save Dargan from that, as Steve Thatcher had promised to do, meant unmasking Sid McEwen! . . . . Impossible both ways!

Steve Thatcher squirmed behind the wheel of the roadster as the full force of his dilemma struck him.

He realized now why Sid McEwen's record was no better than it was. It was good, but it did not compare with Gil's. Gil was incorruptible, a grim servant of the law. Sid was in with crooks—a crook himself. Sid's record showed that in gathering evidence he was weak. His arrests didn't stick. His crooks were released, or they skipped bail and were never found. Steve Thatcher knew why now.

Sid McEwen was in the machine; he'd been bought.

"Great Lord!" Steve Thatcher moaned . . . .

STEVE'S car slowed as he thought things over. His face was hard, his lips pressed grimly together. He checked over what he knew.

Fact: Sid McEwen, forced by Judge Benjamin, had set the trap to kill Beekin—*had* killed Beekin—had stolen the ex-district attorney's notes. Fact: Sid McEwen was using those notes to blackmail Judge Benjamin. Therefore, Sid McEwen had those notes hidden somewhere.

Fact: as long as Sid's guilt remained hidden, it meant the chair was menacing Ned Dargan . . . . Fact: if Sid's guilt was disclosed, it meant heartbreak for Gil McEwen and Sue, a destructive scandal in the force . . . .

Steve Thatcher alone knew the facts. And to act upon them meant a risk for himself—a risk that he would be discovered as the Moon Man.

But he decided . . . .

He pressed the gas-pedal and his roadster shot along the street. He turned corners, raced across intersections, and at last swung into the darkness of an alleyway which flanked an apartment building six stories high. He drew to a stop in the shadows and looked up the sheer brick wall.

Sid McEwen lived in this place, in a suite of rooms four stories up. A fire-escape zigzagged on the side of the building. It did not pass the rooms which Sid McEwen occupied. Yet, there was a way.

Steve Thatcher inched the roadster forward until it was under the lowest platform of the fire-escape. He crawled onto the top, bracing himself on its supports. Grasping the raised ladder, he swung himself, hooked a knee, drew himself up.

He began to climb, silently, like a black cat. Four floors up he paused, on a dark platform. Through the window on the platform he looked into blackness. The apartment inside was empty at the moment. He tried the window. Locked.

Again his glass-cutter and suction cup came into play. He unlatched the window, slid it open, slipped in. He did not even glance at the room as he crossed to the hallway door. Uncatching it, he slipped outside.

The next door opened to Sid McEwen's rooms. It, too, was locked. From Steve Thatcher's pocket came a key. He tried it in the lock, twisting it carefully, adjusting its position. Suddenly it turned. He stepped inside, into darkness again.

He had been in this place a number of times with Sid. A bedroom opened off to the left, a living-room on the right. In it Sid had a flat-top desk. Steve Thatcher crossed the room toward it, and tried its drawers. They were also locked.

Before he tackled the locked drawers, Steve Thatcher glanced around the room. The stolen notes might be hidden in some other place, but this was the most likely. Sid had not had time, so far, to seek a more secure place for them. Steve Thatcher brought out his keys again, and selected a flat, notched one.

Krrrring!

The shrill clatter of the telephone broke the silence. Steve Thatcher froze, staring at the instrument which sat on the desk. It rang again. Quickly he thrust his key into the lock of the center drawer.

Then—a rattle!

It came from the vestibule! Someone was unlocking the outer door! Even at that second a glow of light appeared as the door began to open!

STEVE THATCHER whirled a glance about the room. In the opposite wall was a door. He darted to it, jerked it open. Behind it lay a closet. He slipped inside, closed the door silently.

Steps came into the living-room. A light-switch clicked loudly. A line of white appeared in the darkness at Steve Thatcher's feet, a gleam shining through the crack.

Krrrring!

It was the telephone again. Footfalls answered its summons. The hook clacked as the receiver was lifted. A voice said:

"Hello?"

It was Sid McEwen's voice. He went on speaking in monosyllables.

"Got it, have you? All right, tonight . . . . Where? W h y out there . . . . Yes, I know where it is—right on the shore. What time? . . . . Right. I'll make it. I'll have the stuff with me, but I'm not worrying—you can't get away with anything. Okay!"

The hook clacked again as the receiver went down. A moment of silence followed.

Then there was another, gentler click, and a sliding sound. Steve Thatcher lowered himself and peered through the keyhole of the closet door. He saw Sid McEwen sitting at the desk, opening the drawers.

From a lower drawer Sid McEwen removed a heavy paper envelope, large and tied with coarse ribbon. He opened it, and slid from it a pack of papers. Quickly he began to run through them. Once he paused and drew out a sheet. He read it carefully, his face growing hard.

He struck a match, held the sheet in the flame, watched the fire leap up, and dropped it, smoking, into an ash-tray.

He continued to run through the papers. Soon he finished, and slipped them all back into the red paper envelope. He tied it, rose, and lifted his automatic from his pocket holster. He inspected it carefully.

He tucked the big envelope under his arm, slipped the gun back into its holster, and strode across the room. The lights snapped out. The outer door opened and closed.

Steve Thatcher slipped out of the closet. He crossed the room quickly, to the light-switch, and pressed it. It was a risk: but he had to take the risk. Bending over the desk, he inspected the charred paper in the ash-tray.

It had been covered with typewriting, and all of it was not consumed. Steve Thatcher could make out the heading, and part of the first few lines. It said:

SIDNEY McEWEN

In the employ of Judge Benjamin. His job to prevent Benj .... crowd from interference by the polic .... tips off on raids, prevents .... stool-pigeon for Benjamin ....

Beekin had had the dope on Sid McEwen!

Quickly Steve Thatcher lifted the burned fragment from the ash-tray. He struck another match and lighted it again. It would all go this time. Leaving it flaming in the tray, he strode across the room, snapped off the lights, and slipped out the door . . . .

It was a walk-up apartment. Steve Thatcher did not walk down: he ran. When he reached the lowest floor, he heard the sound of a starter grating outside. He waited until he heard the motor accelerate.

Then he slipped into the open. He saw a car pulling away, its red tail-light gleaming. Sid McEwen was in it . . . . Quickly Steve Thatcher ducked into the alleyway, scrambled into his roadster. He started it swiftly, backed out of the alley, and shot after the car being driven by Sid McEwen.

The red tail-light of the car ahead guided him.

CHAPTER IV

BLACK RENDEZVOUS

IN the chief's office in police headquarters the telephone rang. Gil McEwen was pacing back and forth across the carpet. He grabbed at the phone, pressed the receiver to his ear.

"McEwen talking!"

"Mac! This is King! God, they've got Miss Beekin!"

"What?" McEwen barked the word. "What? Miss Beekin? Who? What's happened?"

"Let me tell you!" The detective sergeant on the other end of the wire was gasping for breath. "I was watching the house, like you told me, to make sure the girl was safe.

Somebody must've got onto me. I was out near the garage when somebody jumped on me from behind. Two men—gorillas!"

"Talk fast!"

"They socked me on the head! I went out! I didn't know what was happening for a time. When I began coming to, I heard somebody on the front porch of the house. I beat it that way—so damn' dizzy I didn't know what was happening. But I saw those two gorillas dragging the girl from the house!"

"Who were they?"

"I don't know! Masked! But they got her! Dragged her out to a car. I went after 'em with the gun. They popped me—both of 'em shooting at once. One of 'em got me in the shoulder—it's busted, Gil. God, it hurts! . . . . They must've thought I was dead. As they started off, I heard one of 'em say to the other, 'Now beat it for the lake'."

" 'The lake'! Sure of that?"

"Yes. It must mean—"

"Rockfall Lake is the only big one around here! By damn! Judge Benjamin's got a cottage on that lake, hasn't he?"

"Right! Only—"

"Get back here and get your shoulder dressed, King! I'll handle the rest of it! I'm beating it out to the lake, to Judge Benjamin's cabin —and I'm taking the whole damn' force with me—as many of 'em as I can get hold of!"

McEwen jerked to his feet, staring dumfoundedly across the room.

"By damn!" he exploded.

He burst out the door, forgetting his hat, and sprang down the stairs, shouting.

BLACKNESS covered the open country, hovered thick over the tar road that stretched into the hills. Along it a car was racing. Sid McEwen was in it, and he had the gas-button pressed to the floor. His white-knuckled hands gripped the wheel as he sent the car careening around bends, climbing higher . . . .

A mile behind, speeding dangerously over the road with its lights out, was another car. Steve Thatcher was in that one. His gaze was directed straight ahead, at the spot of crimson on the road which marked the position of Sid McEwen's car. He did not let it gain on him. His motor was revolving at its limit.

He swerved around the bend, while McEwen's car was lost from sight. Suddenly he saw the red star again, still travelling fast. It was shooting along a branch road now, heading for Rockfall Lake. Then it became clear to Steve Thatcher.

Judge Benjamin had a cabin on Rockfall Lake. Sid McEwen was heading for it—a rendezvous in which the deal would be completed, precious papers traded for a huge sum of money! That was what the telephone conversation, which Steve Thatcher had overheard while hiding in the closet, had meant! Judge Benjamin had been making the appointment.

Steve Thatcher's mind flashed to another scene: himself, in the Moon Man regalia, crouched outside the window of the Judge's study; voices reaching him from inside. Judge Benjamin speaking over the telephone:

"I've got another little job to do; but I'll handle it myself."

And the judge had pocketed an automatic after saying it!

The cold wind penetrated to Steve Thatcher's heart as he whizzed over the road. Now Sid McEwen's car had shot out of sight again, winding its way over the narrow road which skirted the rocky-walled lake. Steve Thatcher sped after it. He glimpsed the red gleam again— saw it moving slowly, drawing off the side of the road.

In the glare of Sid McEwen's headlamps stood a gaunt, black cabin on the edge of the water.

Swiftly Steve Thatcher clicked off the ignition and pressed on the brakes. Risking a collision with rocks and tree-stumps in the darkness, he swung the car off the side of the road, letting it run under its own momentum. Stopped, he watched through the trees.

Down at the shore, the lights of Sid McEwen's car cast a glow over the cabin. Steve Thatcher saw Sid get out of the car. Then the lights snapped out. Steve kept watching. Soon a square of light appeared— the door, opening. Sid McEwen's form was silhouetted an instant before the door closed.

Steve Thatcher paused, grim. This was not for him in his office as detective sergeant! He must show no official knowledge of Sid McEwen's guilt—for Gil's and Sue's sake. He could not, as Steve Thatcher, detective, act to save Ned Dargan. Only as the Moon Man could he do that!

He unlocked the rumble compartment of his roadster, dragged out the overnight case, opened it. In the darkness he drew the black cloak upon himself. He adjusted on his head the spherical mask of Argus glass. Its padding settled it firmly in place; the deflector fitted to the shape of his nose shot his breath downward and outward to keep it from fogging the glass. The mask looked like a mirror-ball, but Steve Thatcher could see through it as though it did not exist at all.

Drawing on his black gloves, he hurried toward the cabin. Bushes tore at his long cloak. He stumbled over roots. He hurried . . . .

Suddenly he stopped short.

Three shots rang sharply in the black silence!

THE reports had come from the cabin—that was a certainty.

The black figure of the Moon Man hurried forward again. Rapidly he reached the clearing in which the cabin sat. It was dark; its windows were covered on the inside, and not the merest glimmer of light

THE SILVER SECRET undefined

shone through. The Moon Man leaped across the open space and pressed close to the log wall of the cabin.

From inside came a muffled voice. "No, there's no danger! There's nobody on the lake at this time of the year! No other cabin is occupied. Nobody could 've heard the shots!"

It was Judge Benjamin speaking. "What about—" It was a gruffer, lower tone now. "We'll handle her the same as we're going to handle him. She knows too much!"

Her—she!

The Moon Man's silver head turned slowly. At least two men were inside. Further mutterings told him there were three. Then there was a low, pitiful wail—the muffled cry of a girl!

Through the slit in the side of his cape, the Moon Man's black-gloved hand slipped—gripping an automatic.

He turned swiftly, toward the rear of the cabin. Rounding the corner, he paused, at a door. In the gloom he could see a hasp and padlock fastening it. He moved again, to a thin crack between the logs of the rear wall, and peered through. Darkness. There were several rooms in the cabin; the rear ones were unlighted; the men and the girl were in the front.

The Moon Man whirled back to the door, drawing through the opening in his cape his bunch of skeleton keys. His silver head bent as he fitted a flat one into the padlock. He tried again; and the padlock clicked open. A sign came from the silver head as the Moon Man slowly inched the door open.

He stepped into the kitchen of the hut, and paused, closing the door behind him. Again he heard voices:

"Hurry up—wire those weights onto him! I'll handle the girl!"

"God, boss, you ain't goin' to croak her here!"

"She knows too much to live! If she was ever called as a witness we'd all be finished!"

Again the Moon Man heard the low, agonized wail.

Silently, a black ghost, he moved toward the connecting door. His black-gloved hand pressed against it. He swung it open slowly. For the merest fraction of a second he surveyed the scene in the room beyond.

Sid McEwen was lying on the floor, motionless, a pool of red under him! Beside him were a pile of rusty sash-weights and a tangle of wire. Two men, burly, thick-necked, were stooping, beginning to wire the weights to the arms and legs of Sid McEwen!

Judge Benjanim, wearing a felt hat pulled low and a bulky top-coat, was standing with his back turned partly to the door. He had a gun in his hand. He was facing the far corner, levelling the gun.

On a cot in the corner a girl was lying. Her silken ankles were bound together, her hands fastened behind her. Over her face a gag was tied. Her eyes were opened wide, in terror, staring at the towering figure of Judge Benjamin.

Barbara Beekin!

THE Judge spoke: "I think you understand, young woman. You're never going to tell all you know. You and this damn' fool are going to the bottom of the lake together. You'll never be found. In a month the water will be frozen over. By spring—"

An inarticulate cry of terror came from the girl.

The Moon Man's mottled, silver head flashed in the light of the lanterns which illumined the room.

"Gentlemen!" he said.

The sound of his voice was a thunderclap in the room. Judge Benjamin whirled. The two men straightened, stared.

They saw, standing in the doorway, facing them, the black-cloaked, silver-headed Moon Man—levelling a gun at them!

"Back away!" the Moon Man ordered.

For one short instant the men in the room were paralyzed with amazement. Terror filled their eyes. Wrathful desperation colored the features of Judge Benjamin.

A shot blasted. A hot slug, spashed with fire, sped from the gun in Judge Benjamin's hand.

The Moon Man leaped aside.

Then a rattling of gun-fire shook the room. Judge Benjamin's gun spoke again. The weapon in the black-gloved hand of the Moon Man blazed with furious flame. The two brutish men who had been bending over Sid McEwen leaped away, drawing revolvers. Slugs splintered into the log walls. Powder-smoke gushed into the lantern-lighted air.

A scream — from Judge Benjamin.

His two helpers whirled, as the Moon Man darted along the rear wall, gun still levelled. A lantern tipped, rolled, went out as the scurrying feet of one of the two men struck it, kicked it aside. The Moon Man heard one of them gasp:

"Beat it!"

They lunged against the front door of the cabin, and out. The Moon Man saw them go, but he made no move to follow. He heard them race off into the darkness, but he kept facing Judge Benjamin.

The Judge was raised slightly on tiptoes, gasping, tottering. His face was a ghastly white. He shoved his gun toward the Moon Man and tried to fire again: but the paralysis of death was upon him. He swung forward—crashed down.

As he rolled over, his top-coat flew open, disclosing a bulging packet of papers in its inside pocket.

The Moon Man stood motionless.

Then suddenly a bright flash of light came from outside, through the partly opened door. Shouts sounded. Pistols cracked, shattering the quiet. The sound of running footfalls came from the road.

"Get 'em! Drop 'em!"

Again guns blasted.

The Moon Man scarcely heard the reports. He thought of nothing now but the voice of the man he had heard shouting, issuing the grim order. He knew that voice—knew it well!

It was Gil McEwen's!

CHAPTER V
STAINED WITH BLOOD

SWIFTLY the Moon Man crossed to the door. He slammed it shut, held it. Turning, he looked at the bound girl on the cot. She was staring at him, wide-eyed—staring with eyes that might see too much!

The black figure paused, turning swiftly. On the near wall of the cabin hung an Indian rug. The black-gloved hand of the Moon Man snatched it down, tearing it off the nails that supported it. He flung it, spreading it over the girl on the cot, covering her face. Now she could not see . . . .

More shots cracked outside. Swift footfalls crashed through the bushes around the cabin. Gil McEwen's voice shouted again:

"Surround it! Hold those guys and watch the cabin!"

The Moon Man's movements were lightning-swift now. He stooped, snatched the packet of papers from the coat-pocket of Judge Benjamin. Whirling, he thrust them under the body of Sid McEwen, near one of Sid's lax hands. Quickly, again, he loosened the wire bound around one of Sid's ankles. He flung it aside, into the fireplace.

Gil McEwen's voice called outside: "Steady! Don't let anybody get out of that cabin!"

The Moon Man straightened. His breath hissed inside his globular glass mask. He could hear men moving all around the shack. He could not get out now. There was no way.

He sped across the room again, and slammed open a door. The small room beyond was dark; but in the gloom he could see, faintly, two beds. He swung the door shut and lifted off his head the sphere of Argus glass.

Swiftly he wriggled out of his black cloak, slipped off his black gloves. The Moon Man vanished; Steve Thatcher, detective sergeant, appeared. Quickly he bundled the robe around the glass ball, and stowed them under the bed. He turned, slipped out of the room again, into the light.

Gil McEwen yelled: "Cover the doors!"

Steve Thatcher waited a moment, for quiet. He gave an answering shout:

"Gil! Come in! It's Steve Thatcher!"

A quick exclamation of surprise answered his call. Heavy heel-beats sounded on the porch, came to the door. The door burst open; and in the light Gil McEwen stood, grim-faced, levelling an automatic.

Steve Thatcher faced him. "Good Lord, Gil! You're here in good time! Did you get those two gorillas?"

"Yeah, we got 'em!"

Gil McEwen was a bit uncertain. Behind him appeared three other men, two in plain clothes, one in uniform. They stared around, saw the cot in the corner, the Indian rug moving. One of them jerked it off.

The girl stared up.

"There she is!"

"Untie her!" McEwen demanded.

He advanced to the center of the room, staring down at the figure on the floor—the body of Sid McEwen, his brother. He raised his eyes to stare at Steve Thatcher. Irrationally, he snapped out another order:

"Look all through this place! Make it quick!"

Steve Thatcher said quietly: "It's Sid, Gil. He got it."

"Sid?"

Gil McEwen looked down again. He stooped, turned the limp form of his brother face up. A grimace of pain crossed his face. Automatically he picked up the bundle of papers.

"That's the stuff stolen from Beekin's tenement room," Steve Thatcher explained quickly. "I can tell you how it happened, Gil. You had Sid watching Judge Benjamin. Sid saw Benjamin leave his house and followed him out here. He phoned me at headquarters, and I followed later. He told me to meet him near the cabin—I tried to find him and couldn't.

"Then I heard shots. I came over here—burst in. Just in time to see Judge Benjamin folding up, and Sid staggering with bullets in him. Sid had got the dope on the Judge. I didn't know then Sid was dead. It looked bad for me—with the two gorillas coming at me. Then they heard you coming, and beat it—lost their nerve."

"By damn!" Gill McEwen burst out.

"Sid's the man who ran this thing down, Gil. He spotted Benjamin—and he got the stolen stuff. He saved the girl, too. It's a tough break, Gil —but we've got to hand it to him."

"Yeah," Gil McEwen said, very soberly.

The door of the rear bedroom swung open. A plain-clothes man hurried out. In his hands he was carrying a bundle—a black bundle! Partly unwrapped, it disclosed the silver mask of the Moon Man!

"Found it under the bed!" the detective exclaimed. "The Moon Man's been here!"

Gil McEwen stared, swung on Steve Thatcher. "You see him?"

"He must 've been here," Steve Thatcher answered quickly. "But he's gone now—he's got away again!"

Gil McEwen's jaws clamped. He stooped, lifted the right hand of Judge Benjamin, and peered at the broad ball of the thumb.

"His print doesn't match. The judge wasn't the man. By damn!" He swung to his men. "Scour the woods! Hunt for him! Stop every car! If the Moon Man's still in this neighborhood, you've got to find him!"

The detective who had found the Moon Man's regalia pushed the cloak and mask into Gil McEwen's hands. The others scattered before him, hurrying out the door. Barbara Beekin was rising from the cot, rubbing her wrists, staring around bewilderedly. Gil McEwen paid her no attention.

He peered at the cloak and mask in his hands; and his gaze dropped to the still figure of his brother.

"Sid was a good guy," he said solemnly. "A good guy—"

"He got his man," Steve Thatcher said.

A HUGE black safe sat in the office of the chief of police. Its doors were swung wide open. Gil McEwen was standing in front of it.

In his hands he was holding again the black cloak and the glass mask of the Moon Man.

"He'll never use 'em again!"

He opened a drawer of the safe, and stuffed the mask and cape into it. He closed the door and locked it.

"He'll have a hell of a time getting another mask like that—if he can get one at all! His hash is settled. He got away, but he won't be able to operate again, without showing himself now!"

Steve Thatcher nodded slowly.

Sue McEwen was standing behind them. She forced a laugh.

"Life for any of us won't be worth living until you've got the Moon Man, Dad," she said. "I do hope you arrest him soon!"

Steve Thatcher winced. It was quite the other way around. Life wouldn't be worth living for him if the Moon Man were ever discovered!

"At least," he said, "we know now that Dargan didn't kill Beekin. He couldn't 've done it— couldn't have locked himself in after he was knocked out, and he certainly wouldn't have done it beforehand. Besides, we've looked all through Beekin's papers, and we don't find Dargan's name mentioned. The other bear traps we found in Benjamin's cabin proved he engineered it—with the help of one of his gorillas."

"Naw," McEwen said. "He wasn't mixed up in it. I saw that right away, and let him ride. But he's being watched. I still think he's connected with the Moon Man—I'm still banking on it that he'll lead me to that damn' crook!"

Steve Thatcher brightened. "You've already let Dargan go?"

"Sure. Just didn't bring him back. He thinks he's escaped, I guess. Well, he can stay out—but he'll stay watched, and damn' close!"

Sue McEwen put a slender hand in Steve Thatcher's.

"Now, Steve," she said, "you're free. You're coming home with me, and we're going to have a little time together again!"

"Delighted!" Steve said. "But wait just a minute. I—I've something to do."

Before she could protest, he hurried out the door. He ran down the stairs, crossed the street, entered the little cigar store on the corner, and wriggled into a booth. Hurriedly he called that very private number.

"Angel!"

"Yes, boss!"

"You're cleared, Angel. The cops won't be coming after you."

www.ingramcontent.com/pod-product-compliance
Lightning Source LLC
Chambersburg PA
CBHW030538180626
46810CB00005B/1920